About the Author

Eric 'ERod' Rodriguez is a content creator and convention host, best known for creating The Blockbuster Buster.

Kassandra Killjoy
Paranormal Private Eye

The Search for the Swordsman

Eric 'ERod' Rodriguez

Kassandra Killjoy
Paranormal Private Eye

The Search for the Swordsman

Pegasus

Chapter 1

Obscure City: The City that Always Creeps

The wind of Obscure City can cut most people with a knife, even on the calmest night at the lowest level of the city. The most average citizen, even after bundling up in their finest fur and hat, would still find that the cold strikes them to the centre of their soul, yet they would just dismiss the cold, dry air as one of the disadvantages of a chilled December night, even when that chilled December night happens to be June. They dismiss all evidence that the chill is not organic in nature but stems from a breeding ground of all those things that go unnoticed to those with a blind eye; those things that define evil, sulk within shadows, stalk behind the corner, and kneel behind a dumpster in a dark, wet alley.

Yet the imminent dangers of this sinister city are unapparent: a peaceful silence has overtaken Obscure this particular evening as every man, woman and child has now retired to their domiciles and every creep to his crypt, leaving the streets dark and desolate. No one will be present to hear the calming quiet of this evening being broken by a long and silky, black and white cat frantically running down the wet sidewalk as if its nine lives depended on it. And no one will be there to witness the four prominent men in pursuit of the feline, who get closer and closer with every stride they take.

The four men are gaining on the black and white cat as it starts to lose its stride. Although all four men are equally intimidating — each large and boasting terrorising muscles and menacing faces — one of the men is substantially larger than the rest in both size and height. The man is known as Kanis Veil, the undisputed leader of the pack of men who are running after the cat. Veil is a man who has no qualms with his hunger for power, or anything else for that matter. He is tall and his imposing muscles bulge out within the confines of his coat. He has long, stringy, unkempt hair that covers the back of his neck, and sideburns that run down both sides of his lantern jaw. His long, black, billowy coat flaps ferociously in the wind as he runs against it.

The cat rounds the corner and makes its way down an alley at full speed until it comes to a screeching halt upon reaching its destination.

At the end of the alley and directly in front of the cat, is a comic-book store. The cat begins frantically scratching at the door of the shop, to no avail.

Veil and his entourage catch up with the cat and begin to slow their pace as soon as they realise the feline is trapped, and begin to inch closer and closer to the helpless animal. The more fear the feline shows, the more they begin taking leisurely paces towards it, as well as pleasure in seeing the fear behind the animal's eyes.

Veil looks down upon the cat and in a chilling voice, begins to speak.

"End of the line, you impure abomination! It's time you learned what happens to your kind when you trespass onto our turf."

The cat lowers his head, puffs out his tail and with his ears back, lets out a bellow.

Suddenly, a woman's voice echoes through the alley and stops the men in their tracks. "Awe… But you're not in your turf any more, boys."

Veil and his men look around frantically for a clue as to where the voice is coming from, when one of the men sees a sign in front of them that informs him just where the pursuit of the feline landed them. The man points up and with a shaky voice exclaims, "Boss look!"

Veil raises his head to see the sign above the door. As he reads, he begins to mentally process his situation. His forehead becomes ribbed, and his eyes widen when he realises the sign says, "Killjoy Komics".

"Ah, crap!" Veil doesn't waste any time and gestures for his men to fall back slowly.

"Kanis Veil." The female voice falls down upon their frightened ears yet again.

The men look up to see a figure standing on the roof of the comic-book store. Kassandra Killjoy stands atop the structure, majestic and confident, while the moonlight silhouettes her figure. Her trench coat and long, braided pigtails flap in the wind, like silk curtains. A blue, wide-brim hat adorns her head and casts a mysterious shadow over half of her face, making her seem even more ominous to the men below.

"You're in my turf now," Killjoy continues. "So do yourself a favour and leave the kitty alone; turn around, and take your three little puppies with you."

The men exchange amused and confused glances and mutter, "Puppies?"

"Or else I'm going to have to take all of you to obedience school. Like good little doggies."

"Stay out of this, Killjoy!" Veil snaps. "This is none of your business!"

"Oh, I think it is."

With this, Killjoy positions herself at the edge of the building and with one quick movement, she leaps forward in the air and lands perfectly balanced in a kneeling position on the concrete ground, under the bright light of a street lamp. As she raises her body to stand equal to the men, their colossal frames cast a shadow on her pale face that fails to darken her bright, lavender-coloured eyes.

Now that she is no longer silhouetted, Veil's henchmen get a good look at her for the first time. They snicker and smirk with delight at her appearance.

Killjoy is wearing a traditional, wide-brimmed, witch's hat and matching coat over a stereotypical 1940's detective suit. She sports a pair of black trousers that don't quite reach her ankles, leaving her black and blue-striped stockings exposed between the hems of her trousers and the top of her high-top sneakers. Covering most of her torso is a blue vest that is not only complementary to her ensemble, but is functional: it holds her pocket watch and its bright, silver chain adorns the front of her raiment. Her appearance is completed by the black and blue tie that she wears in the tradition of those who have shared her profession.

"Now, are you boys gonna scat? Or do I have to get a rolled up newspaper?"

Veil's voice is filled with disdain. "Listen to me, you half-breed piece of—"

Before Veil can finish his sentence, Killjoy makes an old fashioned wooden broom appear in her hand with a simple flick of her wrist. Veil and his goons flinch and step back, being careful with their movements. Veil's goons are no longer amused and now take a serious stance as their fight-or-flight instincts begin to kick in. They anxiously await orders from their leader, who holds his ground with unshakable determination.

Killjoy grips the broom tightly in her hand, while making eye contact with Veil. "This is your last warning, Veil. Otherwise you're going to leave this alley without one of your pups."

The goons make sure that Veil isn't looking in their direction as they exchange nervous glances.

"Easy to talk tough while you're holding that!" Veil smirks, as he points to the broom.

"Oh, I don't need this to beat you." And with that, Killjoy lets go of the broom. The broom miraculously remains upright as if being held up by an invisible force. "All I need… is this."

Killjoy pulls out an antique change purse from the pocket of her vest. She dramatically drops the purse on the ground. The change purse hits the concrete floor with so much force that coins can be heard rolling inside it and the sound sends a cautionary echo throughout the alley.

Veil and his men are noticeably annoyed by Killjoy's display of bravado, but remain stoic. Veil curls his lip into a sinister smile. "You shouldn't have let go of your broom."

The three men then outstretch their arms and their chests expand. They begin to morph quickly and painlessly as Killjoy watches on. Their mouths gape and their eyes widen and flash red; their clothing begins to rip as their muscles grow larger; their bodies grow hairy and their statures increase to five times their human size. Upon completion of their transformation, Killjoy finds her gaze drifting even further upward to take in the sight of three werewolves.

"Take her!" Veil commands.

The black and white cat watches in astonishment as two of the werewolves charge at Killjoy at full speed.

Killjoy, however, remains still and confident. She allows the two werewolves to close the distance between them as she patiently waits.

When the first werewolf gets to five feet from her, Killjoy throws a small, wooden talisman at his chest.

"Madera Maxima!" Killjoy commands.

Suddenly every scrap of wood littering the alley begins to fly through the air, encapsulating the werewolf, completely trapping him in a four-walled dog house.

The second werewolf, having been distracted by the extraordinary event, turns his head around to see his fellow werewolf trapped in wood, but before he has an opportunity to turn back around and see what Killjoy is doing, she is already in front of him. Before he can react, she slaps a strange metal device onto his face. The sudden attack and force causes the werewolf to fall to the ground with a sickening thud. The werewolf tries to get the device off of his face but every time he claws at it or scratches it, the device contorts and snaps into place, causing it to become a more elaborate muzzle, forcing his enormous jaw shut. In spite of this, he continues to fiddle with the device, which makes his situation worse and worse.

Killjoy, satisfied with her work, displays a smile but only for a second. The third werewolf is in mid-flight and seconds away from pouncing on her. She does not have time for spells or tricks and quickly shoulder rolls out of the way to avoid the werewolf's claws by mere inches. The werewolf approaches with his mouth wide open. Killjoy quickly grabs the change purse from the ground and throws it directly into the werewolf's mouth with enough speed and precision to propel it down the unwilling werewolf's throat. He is only perturbed by the occurrence for a moment. He shakes it off and gets ready to attack again, when he is suddenly stopped by a loud gastrointestinal sound coming from his stomach. He howls in pain and drops to the ground while holding onto his midsection.

Veil and the black and white cat watch in shock as the werewolf is forcefully morphed back into his human form and green flames shoot out of his stomach. Soon the green fire consumes his body, leaving nothing but ash.

Veil stares in disbelief as he enquires, "What was in that purse?"

"Ten silver coins," Killjoy answers.

"You half-blood bitch!" Veil angrily exclaims as he morphs into his werewolf form, which is twice the size of his subordinates and far grizzlier by comparison. He runs at Killjoy with all the speed he can muster and fully intending to tear her to shreds.

Killjoy effortlessly takes a side step and lets him run past her via his own momentum. She quickly pulls her pocket-watch out of her vest and wraps the chain around Veil's neck like a dog's leash. The chain magically expands about five feet beyond its normal length, until Killjoy gives it a firm tug. Veil is suddenly jerked back by his neck and hits the ground hard; in the process, he nearly cracks the back of his head on the pavement.

"Sit, Boo-Boo. Sit!" Killjoy says in a brassy tone, without losing grip of the chain.

Smoke begins emanating from the chain around Veil's neck as he changes back to human form.

"Just in case you were wondering, that chain is also made of out of silver."

"You stupid—"

Killjoy pulls on the chain, cutting his words short. "God, I wish I had my phone right now. I would love to send the rest of your clan a picture of me taking you out for walkies."

Veil tries to talk but the chain around his neck prevents him from doing so.

"Now, Veil — take your last two pups and go back to your turf and stay there. I officially pronounce this black and white cat as my familiar. So, if I ever catch you messing with it again, I'll put ten silver coins inside you. And when I do, I promise I will use the rear exit… If you know what I mean."

Veil's eyes widen as he knows exactly what she means.

With this, Killjoy releases him and Veil pathetically falls to the ground. She turns around and goes to check on the cat.

Once she does, Veil, furious beyond reason, goes to attack her once more.

"Die, you half-breed wench"

With a slight gesture, Killjoy makes the broom fly into her hand. A second later, a bright green flash and a very loud bang can be heard throughout the city. Veil flies out of the alley, and slams into a parked car which heavily dents the entire side of the vehicle.

Killjoy is standing in the entrance of the alleyway, holding her broom like a shot gun. *Bang,*" she says with a satisfied jerk of her head.

With a simple hand gesture, Killjoy frees the two trapped werewolves. They pathetically stumble out of the alley to help Veil back on his feet, and they run away together.

After they leave, Killjoy walks back into the alley. Once she gets close to the cat, she reaches into her vest pocket and procures her pocket-watch, which magically becomes a magnifying glass that she uses to examine the feline. "Now, what's so special about you Salem? Do you poop gold nuggets? 'Cause if that's the case, I'm buying a litter box tonight!"

At that moment, the black and white cat responds in a deep velvety voice that doesn't quite match his small frame. "Hey Lady, you gots any tuna oveh deh?"

Killjoy looks at the creature with her mouth agape. "Oh, this officially got really interesting!"

She quickly procures a business card from her coat pocket and holds it in front of the cat's face, as she introduces herself. "Kassandra Killjoy, Paranormal Private-Eye at your service."

The cat just stares at her blankly.

"What's your name?" Killjoy further enquires, but the cat just sniffs the business card, completely ignoring her query. "Hey Lady, these am not tunas."

Killjoy takes an exasperated breath, but suddenly notices the name tag hanging from the cat's collar: it reads Hime. Killjoy raises her eyebrows at the peculiar appellation.

"Well, that's a unique name. So, Hime, what was so urgent that was worth nearly getting eaten by werewolves?"

As she says this she notices a USB drive hanging from Hime's collar, right behind his name tag. Killjoy carefully removes the drive from the collar and looks at it through her magnifying glass.

"That for you, lady," Hime clarifies. "You take that and give me the tunas."

"Well, Hime, I have to hand it to you: you are consistent."

Killjoy looks at the USB drive with an extreme amount of interest.

Chapter 2

Killjoy Komics: Private Eye for Hire

As Killjoy and Hime walk into the comic-book store, a bell chimes. The smell of plastic, cardboard and dust fills the air. There are shelves on each side lined with the newest releases, and boxes on long tables filled with musty back issues organised alphabetically by title. Statues, collectables, and figurines with price tags are displayed in a case with a lock, towards the middle of the store. Behind the counter stands Killjoy's only employee, affectionately referred to as Dan The-Comic-Book-Man. Dan's lanky body is leaning on the counter, one hand on his face while he flips through the inventory list. With a quick glance towards the door, his long, stringy hair moves into his eyes. Upon realising the bell doesn't indicate a customer, he looks back down at his paperwork, unaffected by the cat that is following his boss.

Customers stand around the store, thumbing through comics. Like Dan, none of the patrons seems to be fazed by the presence of Hime as they continue to browse the pages of the books.

Believe it or not, Killjoy thinks, as she closes the door behind her, *this isn't the weirdest way I've ever stumbled upon a new case.* She gives a wry smile. *But that's another story.*

Killjoy looks over at Hime with curiosity. *What matters now is that this little creature bravely risked his life just to ask for my help. That, in itself, deserves my undivided attention.*

Killjoy leads Hime through the store towards Dan.

"Hey, Dan — this is Hime, my new client. Hime, this is Dan The-Comic-Book-Man."

Dan takes his hand off his face and waves at Hime. "S'up cat dude."

"Hey deh Misteh, you gots any tuna oveh deh?" Hime requested.

Dan is completely unfazed by Hime's verbal skills. "Sorry, cat dude. I only gots breakfast bars and Gatorade."

Killjoy shakes her head as she interjects, "Dan, I'm going to take Hime into my office. If any more 'angry puppies' come sniffing around here, make sure to buzz me."

"You got it, Boss. What's up with Veil and the Howling Commandos, anyway?"

"Werewolves, Golden Retrievers, German Shepherds and so on… Dogs are dogs, and they don't like cats."

"Whoa, Boss — that makes, like, all the sense."

With a smirk and a chuckle, Killjoy and Hime make their way to the back of the store into her office. She stops in front of an open door that leads into a small bathroom. Frustrated, Killjoy turns to address the entire store.

"How many times do I have to tell you savages? You're free to use the employee bathroom as long as you remember to close the door when you're done!" Killjoy yells out.

"Sorry," Dan and the others mutter unenthusiastically without taking their eyes off the comics they are reading.

Killjoy rolls her eyes while turning around, and slams the bathroom door shut. Turning the knob in the opposite direction, she reopens it. When the door opens, the room beyond the door is no longer a bathroom, but an office.

"After you, sir."

Hime looks in astonishment as Killjoy ushers him in. "Hey Lady, where did the water room go?"

"Trade secret, little man," she responds, as the door closes behind them.

The room is incredibly cluttered with books, papers, and random knick-knacks scattered about, but it is functional. Shelves are loaded with relics and mementos from Killjoy's previous cases. In contrast to the rest of the room, the desk is organised in meticulous fashion, with only a computer and a table lamp sitting upon it. The lamp emanates a green light, which serves as the only source of light in the room. There is a desk chair at one end and a black leather chair at the other.

Killjoy follows Hime into the room and recklessly tosses her broom to the side, but it lands perfectly on a pair of hooks hanging from the wall.

"Sorry about the mess," Killjoy says, apologetically. "It's the cleaning gnome's day off."

"That's okay, lady. Maybe you give me some tunas for my mouff?" Hime abruptly requests.

Killjoy stares him down with an arched eyebrow while Hime is delightfully unaware of his rudeness.

She lets out an exasperated sigh and procures a can of green beans from a nearby cupboard. Giving the can a shake, it transforms into a can of tuna. It pops open on its own as Killjoy lays it before Hime.

The chatty cat immediately starts to gulp down the tuna, making cartoonish eating sounds, "Yum, yum, yum."

Killjoy shrugs her shoulders and walks over to her desk, plugging the USB drive into the computer as she sits. "Now, let's see if we can get some much needed exposition."

The USB drive, surprisingly, has only one file: a video. When Killjoy double clicks on it, the video starts to play, featuring an average-looking, portly man of Chinese descent. He looks at the camera, addressing Killjoy directly.

"Hello, Ms Killjoy. My name is Charles Chan. While I can't reveal my profession to you, what I can tell you is that it is not that different from your very own. I also deal with Obscure City's more — let's say… interesting citizens on a nightly basis; such as my faithful friend Hime, whom you just met."

Killjoy glances at Hime who continues to chomp away at the tuna.

"If you are watching this, that means I have not returned from my latest case and my daughter, Madeline, has been left alone."

A picture of a young girl appears in the top left corner of the video. Madeline Chan looks to be a Chinese girl, no more than sixteen years old. Having not yet lost the innocence of youth, her face is dotted with tiny freckles on her nose and cheeks. The jet-black hair piled on top of Madeline's head accents her black, goth-like clothing perfectly.

"Ms Killjoy, I can't reveal to you why, but if I'm gone, my daughter is in grave danger. So I would like to hire you to protect her for the next six months. If you check your bank account, adequate compensation has been transferred to you by now."

Pausing the video, Killjoy opens a second window on the computer to check her funds on her online bank.

"Holy Hecate!" she exclaims. "Yes, Charles, I would definitely say that this compensation is more than adequate."

Returning to the video, Killjoy resumes the playback. "Ms Killjoy, please understand that my daughter is still unaware of our world. I'm counting on you to not only keep her safe, but to gently usher her into it as well. She is the most precious part of my life and I would hate for her to get caught in the crossfire caused by the constant squabbling of the Seven Families."

With that, the video abruptly ends. Killjoy arches her brow with intrigue at her client's last words.

"Who are you, Chuck?" She glances at Hime in hope of a response. However, he has now switched from vigorously eating to vigorously licking himself. "It's okay, kitty — you don't have to answer now. I see you're busy," she says with a sigh.

Killjoy relaxes back in her leather chair as the gears in her head begin to turn. "Well, Hime, your boss paid in advance, so I have no choice but to take the case. We'll get to work in the morning. It's been a long night." With that said, Killjoy stands up and Hime stretches, no longer in the throes of self-grooming. They both go to the door and Killjoy turns the knob to convert the office back to the nondescript "employee bathroom".

———

Daytime in Obscure City is in stark contrast to its nightly hours. Hundreds of humans now populate its streets and sidewalks, blindly going about their businesses of daily life. Cars line the streets, and people line the sidewalks, all going about their day completely unaware that if an angel fell or a demon rose, they would probably land on the concrete on which they are now walking.

Like its human citizens, Obscure's resident Paranormal Private-Eye, Kassandra Killjoy, has business of her own to attend to. She walks the cracked sidewalks of her city, accompanied by her new familiar, Hime, as they make their way towards an apartment building, where Charles and Madeline Chan are supposed to reside. Instead of going into the building directly, they stop, and then cross the street to the building directly across from the apartment complex. Hime looks up at Killjoy, both curious and confused as to why they didn't just go into the correct building. However, Killjoy seems to know what she is doing, and both make their way into the stairwell and up the many flights. At the top of the stairs is a door that leads to the very top of the building. Walking outside with Hime by her side, Killjoy pulls a tiny metal fly from her pocket and speaks to it.

"I spy with my little eye — Madeline Chan." As she says the words, the metal fly vibrates and comes to life, opening one eye in the centre of its head. It suddenly flies towards Charles Chan's apartment window, slipping in through a tiny crack between the window and sill. Killjoy draws her magnifying glass from her coat pocket, which quickly reveals an image projected on the surface of the glass.

She looks at the projection intently, and it becomes apparent to Hime that the images are being sent from the metal fly. Killjoy can now see inside Charles' apartment discretely, without having to go inside.

The metal fly hovers around, slowly revealing the interior of the apartment. Pizza boxes, empty soda bottles, and dirty laundry litter the ground, and the kitchen sink is full of dirty dishes. It's apparent that only a teenager has occupied this home for quite some time.

Continuing down the hallway, the fly hovers by a room with the name 'Maddy' written on the door; however, it seems there is no one inside.

The fly moves back into the living room, when suddenly something seems to shift under one of the giant piles of laundry on the sofa. It glides towards the twitching mound of dirty clothes only to discover a person is making these movements. Madeline is sleeping underneath it, using the clothes as a makeshift blanket. Killjoy's fly focuses on the sleeping teen. She is curled up in a tight ball with her hands next to a landline phone, as if she is waiting for an important call and wants it answered quickly.

Suddenly, the alarm from her cell phone goes off. Madeline awakes with a start. She seems disoriented from being awoken from a deep sleep for a moment but quickly gains her composure, reaching over the end table and checking the answering machine.

"You have no new messages." Madeline lets out a groan of frustration as she resigns herself to start getting ready for the day and what Killjoy presumes to be school.

The fly discreetly follows Madeline as Killjoy takes out a notepad and pen from her coat pocket. The pen stands upright on its own following Killjoy's voice and writing her dictation.

"Subject: Madeline Xia Chan. Average student, excellent skateboarder, stubborn daughter. Her father has been missing for over a week, yet she won't stop waiting for a phone call or sign indicating his whereabouts. This fails to arouse the suspicion of her friends and neighbours, as it is very common for Charles to take off on business trips for days at a time. According to the public record, Charles Chan is a travelling businessman with a degree in accounting. This is both true and false. Charles handles all his accounting duties online, and they do not require him to travel. However, he has never been gone this long, and understandably, his daughter is worried. As far as where he goes on these alleged business trips, it is still a mystery, but I feel that discovering this will help shed light on his sudden disappearance and the alleged danger in which Madeline might find herself."

Noticing Madeline getting dressed, Killjoy and Hime begin to make their way down the staircase, anticipating the inevitable departure.

Back inside the apartment, Madeline puts on a black t-shirt with the American Sign Language symbol for 'I love you' on the front. Her jeans are black and baggy, with the knees cut out and a chain dangling from the waist, which she connects to her wallet in her back pocket. She compliments her ensemble by snapping a black choker around her neck.

Once dressed, she grabs her skateboard and backpack and heads out of the apartment. When she gets outside, Madeline takes off on her skateboard, leaving Killjoy to follow at a safe distance. Her peculiar fly continues to keep up while also projecting the events into her magnifying glass. She can stay a safe distance yet be aware of everything going on, and everything said.

Madeline's first stop isn't at school. Instead, she leads Killjoy to the Obscure City Police Department. Madeline walks in and confronts the desk sergeant.

"S'up, Calhoun. Is Detective Lankaster in?"

The sergeant looks up from his computer. "Sorry, Maddy. He got called away on a case. He should be back this afternoon."

Madeline lets out a frustrated sigh and turns to leave. "Fine. I'll be back after school."

"Maddy, he's doing everything he can to find your pop."

Madeline glances back at him with a distrustful glare. "Yeah, right."

Feeling helpless and frustrated, Madeline briskly walks towards the door with her skateboard under her arm. Trying to get out of the place as quickly as possible, she nearly knocks down bystanders.

Once Madeline is out of the building, Killjoy enters and walks up to the service desk. Sergeant Calhoun smiles knowingly and hands Killjoy a large envelope, as she passes him a smaller, yet considerably fatter, envelope which he pockets. She takes the envelope from Calhoun's hand, opening it to reveal a copy of Madeline's records. Killjoy flips through the pages until she stops on the section detailing Madeline's scholastic records. It seems she is currently enrolled at Ray Harryhausen High School.

Killjoy flashes Calhoun a smile, and he gives her an appreciative nod as she makes her way out of the station.

The sun now hangs high in the sky of Obscure city, announcing the arrival of this day's afternoon and indiscriminately casting its rays of illumination on the building where Madeline Chan acquires her education. The large sign on the corner identifying Ray Harryhausen High School stands proudly in front of the facility as a gesture of welcoming warmth to the youth seeking knowledge. Redbrick surrounds a concrete engraving stating, 'Established 1862 Home of the Fighting Tigers'. A tiger's face, the school mascot, is featured in the middle of the sign.

Directly across from the school, with equally as welcoming warmth, the Methodist Church of Obscure City can be found, whose sign reads, 'Established 1860.' It serves as a reminder that humans tend to establish a deity before seeking knowledge. Atop the church sits Killjoy, who continues to watch Madeline through the magnifying glass with a noticeable loss of interest. Hime appears on the church roof, carrying a paper bag in his mouth. Upon his arrival, Killjoy looks up with a start.

"Finally!" she exclaims, taking the bag from him. She pulls two sandwiches out of the bag and lays one before him.

Hime knocks the top bread off his sandwich, revealing tuna inside, and begins chomping away at the fish content, making the same comical sound as before "Yum, Yum, Yum."

Killjoy ravenously takes a bite out of her sandwich but quickly spits it out. "Merciful Malus! I said no pickles! You heard me say 'no pickles' when I called in the order, right?" she questions, turning towards Hime for confirmation. However, just like when they met, his focus remains on the tuna.

"Just another disappointment during a boring day of following—" Her words stop short when she notices a sleek, vintage, black car parking near the school. "Wait a minute. That's no soccer-mom van." Killjoy picks up her magnifying glass, and Madeline's continued surveillance footage fades away. Holding the magnifying glass over her eye, she looks directly at the black car. With a quick hand gesture, she makes the vehicle's image within the glass zoom in. She focuses in on the car's windshield, but due to the heavy tint covering the window, she cannot see the driver. She looks around the rest of the vehicle, trying to find any clues or any indication of the identity of its occupant, when she finally notices a familiar symbol etched onto the hood of the car. The logo is the letter S with an X over its top.

"Oh no…" Killjoy quietly whispers as she swiftly pulls an enormous book out of the small pocket of her coat. Hime is so surprised by the sudden appearance of the hefty tome that it takes his focus away from his meal for a moment — but only for a moment.

Killjoy slams the book down on the top of a roof turbine and begins to flip rapidly through the pages, searching until she finally comes upon the page with the symbol. "Slasher Clan," she reads aloud, with dread in her voice. "And suddenly," she says as she turns to Hime, "pickles are the least of my worries."

Chapter 3

It's a Mad, Mad... Madeline

Detective Lankaster sits at his desk, cluttered with folders packed with active investigations. Tired eyes settle their gaze on one of the open files before him as he takes out a handkerchief from his top pocket and quickly wipes the day's smudges from his glasses. He lets out an exhausted sigh before returning his glasses to the base of his nose.

For every case he can finally put in the 'closed' pile, it feels that three more new cases are there to take their place. His attention focuses on the case file in front of him, when Madeline Chan slings open his door and makes a bee-line up to his desk.

"No, Ms Chan. I have no new leads on your father's case. Rest assured, if and when I find out anything, I will call you."

"Actually, I'm here to tell you to stop looking," Madeline said, matter-of-factly.

Taken aback, Lankaster's eyes rise to meet hers. "Excuse me?"

"Well, obviously, you don't give a crap about my dad. So don't bother."

"Madeline, please. It's not that I don't care. You're not my only case; I have others that require my attention. Families that need our help as much as you do," he tries to reason.

Unfazed, Madeline puts her hand down on the desk, slowly lowering herself so she can look directly into his face. "Good news then, now you have one less family to worry about." With that, she turns on her heels and storms out of the police station before allowing the detective to respond.

Once outside, Madeline pulls her skateboard out of her backpack, taking in a deep breath in a desperate attempt to hold back the stinging bite of her tears she refuses to let fall. She puts her skateboard down, about to propel herself forward, when she hears a woman's voice behind her.

"Hey, kid. You need help finding your old man?"

Madeline turns her head, seeing the owner of the voice, a woman dressed in a black business suit, leaning against the wall of the police station. Nothing about her appearance seems out of the ordinary. Madeline turns the rest of her body to face her with curiosity and confusion behind her eyes. "Excuse me?"

The strange woman reaches in her coat to pull out what looks like a business card, handing it to Madeline. "My name's Kassandra Killjoy, Private Eye."

Madeline, still confused, takes the card. "How did you know about—?"

"Your missing-person case?" Killjoy interrupts. "Sergeant Calhoun gave me the details earlier today. Part of a long-standing tradition of cops and private eyes scratching each other's backs," Killjoy replies with a smile.

"I'll take all the help I can get, but I… I can't pay you anything."

"Don't worry about that right now. We can figure that out later. First, I suggest we go somewhere quiet, where we can talk."

Still in a bit of a confused-like shock, Madeline nods. She opens her mouth to suggest a location when she notices a cat standing next to Killjoy. It's Hime.

"Wait! What are you doing with my dad's cat?"

Taken aback, Killjoy attempts to cover her tracks. "This cat? No, no, no — I've had him for years."

"Oh, really?" Madeline crosses her arms while eyeing Killjoy suspiciously. "Then what's his name?"

Killjoy pauses momentarily, "Keanu?"

The hesitation of Killjoy's answer was all Madeline needed to hear. She starts to walk away.

"Stay away from me, lady!" Madeline yells out.

Taking a step towards her, Killjoy reached her hand in reassurance, "Madeline, please, I—" she stops her plea as she notices two female officers heading their way with determination and purpose. They must have heard Madeline shouting.

"Is there a problem here, miss?" the first officer asks.

"Yeah! This crazy lady is stalking me, and she stole my dad's cat!"

"This is just a misunderstanding—" Killjoy tries to explain, to no avail.

"Ma'am, I will have to ask you to step back," the second officer instructs, as she turns to her partner. "Get the minor out of here." The second officer guides Madeline down an alley next to the building as the other officer continues to block Killjoy's path. "Ma'am, I'm not going to ask you twice," the first officer sternly commands, pulling a pair of handcuffs from her belt. As she does this, Killjoy notices the same SX symbol she had seen on the hood of the black car tattooed on the officer's wrist.

"Son of a—" Killjoy proclaims in annoyance as she pulls her broom out of her coat and holds it over her head. The broom takes flight over the officer's head, pulling Killjoy along.

In the alley, the other officer has Madeline by her shoulder more forcibly than one would expect from a public servant of the law.

"I'm sorry, but where are you taking me?" Madeline demands.

"Back to our master," the officer states, as she guides the young girl towards the end of the alley, just as the black car with the SX symbol on the hood pulls up to meet them.

Realizing the danger, Madeline becomes scared and tries to break herself free, but the imposter officer is too strong.

"Not so fast, Cagney!" Killjoy lands in front of them. Killjoy is no longer wearing her business suit and now sports her usual attire.

"What the hell are you?" Madeline's heart is beating so hard that it nearly drowns out her own words.

"You're in luck, kid," Killjoy gives a wink. "I'm a Witch with enough mystic force at my command to easily dispatch a couple of rent-a-cops." She looks at the imposter. "So, let Madeline go, or I'm going to—"

Suddenly, the other imposter officer sneaks up behind Killjoy, spins her around, and snaps a pair of handcuffs on her.

"Damn — forgot about Lacey," Killjoy quips.

"Stay out of our way, half-witch," the second imposter warns.

"Handcuffs? Really? A Witch can easily escape any bonds!"

The imposter smiles. "Not if they're made of iron."

Killjoy looks down at the handcuffs with concern and tries to pull them apart without success. "Oh, iron… yeah, that… that sucks." The imposter kicks Killjoy into the wall, which cracks the concrete as she tumbles down like a rag doll. "Man! I've forgotten how much pain hurts."

The imposter that took Madeline down the alley tries to put her in the back of the black car, but Madeline sprays her eyes with a can of pepper spray she had hanging from her key chain. The imposter screams in pain as she loosens her grip, and Madeline attempts to run away.

Before she can get too far, the second imposter blocks her path. Madeline holds up her skateboard and gets in position to take a swing at her attacker when, suddenly, the imposter begins to morph into her proper form. A horrified Madeline watches, disbelievingly, as the imposter's skin turns pale and grey, and her face becomes old and scarred. She holds a pair of sickle blades in her hands. Madeline quickly turns her head to see that the other imposter is also similar in appearance; both with scarred faces, grey skin, withered hair, and demonic glowing eyes.

"What the hell are you people?" Madeline demands.

"People? We are not people. We are Rip—"

"And Torn."

"And we will take you back to our master in peace—"

"… or in pieces."

"It's up to you."

The two grotesque women begin to close in on Madeline as they brandish their blades.

Madeline turns to see Killjoy, still on the ground and struggling with the handcuffs. "Help me, please!" she begs.

"I would love to, kid," Killjoy says apologetically, "but iron makes me pretty useless."

Suddenly, Hime lands in front of Killjoy and Madeline and hisses menacingly at the two approaching creatures. "Hey deh Ugly Tings, these are my Persons. They belong to me."

"Did my Dad's cat just talk?" Madeline asked in complete shock.

"It's getting him to shut up; that would be truly amazing." Killjoy answers as she continues to try and free herself from the handcuffs.

Rip and Torn close in on Hime.

"What is this?" Rip asks in amusement.

"An appetizer," Torn replies.

"Before the main course?"

At this, Madeline addresses Killjoy desperately, "Lady, please do something! Anything! These things are going to eat my dad's cat!"

Killjoy hurriedly works on the handcuffs. "I'm… trying!"

Hime suddenly vanishes, which causes everyone to freeze in shock. Then, without warning, Hime reappears on Torn's shoulder. "Hey, lady."

Rip sees Hime and tries to punch him, but he disappears, and she punches her sister instead. Torn crumbles to the ground holding her face.

"You gots any Tunas over deh?" Hime says from behind Rip.

Rip turns to see the feline perched on some wooden pallets. She leaps at Hime, but he disappears, and she flies headfirst into a garbage can.

Madeline and Killjoy watch in complete astonishment.

"My dad's cat can talk and teleport?" Madeline gives Killjoy a shocked glance.

"I'm just as surprised as you, kid." Killjoy reaches into her hair as she says this, pulls out a hairpin, and begins to pick the lock on the handcuffs.

Rip emerges from the trash can, brushes some garbage off herself, and begins heading towards Madeline and Killjoy, steadily and rapidly.

"Lady! Lady!" Madeline exclaims in a panic. "She-monster is coming our way!"

"Okay, first: never panic. Panicking gets you dead, and secondly…" Killjoy undoes one of her bonds, and she quickly stabs Rip in the neck with the open cuff, "my name is Killjoy."

Torn notices that her sister is wounded, and she quickly pulls herself away from her fruitless attempts to catch or hit Hime. She grabs Rip and leads her out of the alley towards the black car. Killjoy finishes unlocking the handcuffs, and she tosses them to the side. Once free of the iron bonds, her hands again flow with magical energy.

"All right. You want to fight dirty, then dirty we shall fight." Killjoy makes her broom take off from the ground with a quick gesture and it lands in her hand. She points the broom at the two fleeing monsters, and just as she is about to fire, loud gunshots echo through the alley. Madeline and Killjoy duck for cover, and Hime dives behind a dumpster. Madeline and Killjoy turn to see Sergeant Calhoun firing his sidearm at Rip and Torn. The terrifying twins get hit by the bullets a few times, but they keep moving and are completely unfazed by their wounds. They quickly jump in the car and take off.

Calhoun stands frozen with the smoking gun still in his hands. "What the hell were those things?"

"Just a couple of Slashers, Cal. Nothing to worry about." Killjoy smiles at the sergeant.

"Damn it, Killjoy! Everywhere you go, weird shit follows." He lets out an exasperated sigh as he puts his sidearm in its holster.

"Eh, it's a living." Killjoy turns to address Madeline, but she is halfway down the alley on her skateboard. "Merciful Malus!" Killjoy tosses her pocket watch at Madeline. The chain stretches far beyond its standard length, wraps itself around Madeline, and yanks her back. Madeline lands with a thud, right in front of Killjoy while her skateboard continues rolling down the alley until it crashes into a chain-linked fence.

Killjoy stands over Madeline. "Look, kid — your dad hired me to protect you. So, you have a choice: you either stick with me and live, or you take off on your own and wait until the next creepy thing pulls you into an alley. So, what's it going to be?"

Later that afternoon, in the Chan's apartment building, Killjoy walks leisurely down the hallway while dragging a non-compliant Madeline behind her. The teen floats through the air inside a green bubble with her arms crossed and bearing an annoyed look on her face. Hime follows them, dragging Madeline's skateboard and backpack along.

While facing forward, Madeline addresses Killjoy in a loud tone. "You know, for someone who is supposed to be my protector, you're certainly acting like a kidnapper!"

"Scream all you want, kid. No one can hear you right now, but me. I'm lucky that way."

"I still think you're overreacting. So, a couple of freaks jumped me in an ally. It doesn't mean there's some kind of conspiracy against me and—" Madeline notices that the door to her apartment has been broken open.

"You were saying?" Killjoy asks snidely.

They enter the apartment with caution to find the place in complete disarray. Items and papers are strewn about, drawers left open. The area does not look as though it has been robbed, but rather, someone was looking for something specific. Killjoy carelessly pops the green bubble, drops Madeline on the living room couch, and begins looking the place over with her magnifying glass.

"Why would someone do this to our apartment?" Madeline asks.

"How can you tell the difference?" Killjoy replies mockingly.

"How do you know what the apartment looked like before?"

"I had you under surveillance for the past two days." Madeline stares at Killjoy in complete shock. "Not in a weird way. I just bugged your apartment and watched you sleep."

Madeline's expression changes from shocked to concerned. "Yeah, totally not in a weird way at all."

Madeline shrugs off her concern with a raised tone. "All right. Fine, crazy witch lady. Could you at least tell me what the hell is going on with my dad?"

"Killjoy."

"What?"

"My name is Killjoy, Madeline. Madeline? Ma-the-line. Ma— man, that is a mouthful. Do you mind if I call you Mad?"

"Yes, I do mind," she replies, intensely annoyed.

"All right, Mad — so your dad sent me a message via your chatty kitty, and he mysteriously claimed that you were in imminent danger. Judging by the fact that a couple of Slashers jumped you, your dad seriously undersold the level of danger that you are in."

"But what could these… 'Slashers' want with me, and my dad? We're nobodies."

"You have something they want."

"What makes you say that?"

"Really? Your ransacked apartment is not enough of a clue?"

"Yeah. But what do they want?"

"Beats me."

"Pffft, great detective you are."

Killjoy is taken aback by Mad's snarky remark. "Really? You want to do this?" Before Mad can respond, Killjoy begins deducing at lightning speed. "The clean break through the four locks on your front door tells me that your intruder has supernatural strength. The crack at the top of the doorframe where he hit his head tells me he is over seven feet tall. The single pair of eighteen-inch footprints tell me he was here alone, and the fact that he stood in this very spot for ten minutes reading the comic strips in your newspaper, all the while he was supposed to be searching your place, tells me he is not very bright." Mad looks at Killjoy with an impressed look on her face. "Do you want me to keep going?"

"All right, all right. I get it. Calm down, Cumberbatch." Mad looks at her broken front door and thinks for a moment. "So, let me get this straight. Monsters and witches… Those things are real?"

"As real as you and me."

"And my dad has something to do with them?"

"Yeah, but don't worry, Mad. I'll figure it out. It's what I do." Killjoy notices the intruder's massive footprints headed into a room down the hallway. "What's in there?"

"Just my dad's office."

Mad and Killjoy enter the office area to find that it has also been searched. Killjoy immediately begins to go through Charles' desk.

"Killjoy, I don't think you'll find anything here. My dad's just a boring old accountant." As she says this, Killjoy presses a secret switch hidden in Charles' desk.

Secret panels slide open in the walls, revealing all matter of supernatural paraphernalia. Mad looks at the contents of these hidden compartments with her mouth agape.

Killjoy gazes at her with a sly smile. "You were saying. . ?"

Suddenly, something catches Killjoy's eye. She quickly walks across the room to a compartment full of medieval weaponry. A metal emblem is displayed in the middle of the weapons, and it has a code of arms painted on the front of it. Killjoy walks up to it in absolute astonishment, takes the emblem from the display and brings it close to her face to inspect it properly.

"Holy Hecate!" Killjoy breathlessly exclaims.

"What? Is my dad into larping?"

"No, Mad. Your dad is The Squire!"

"The what?"

"The Squire." Mad stares at her, wide-eyed and clueless. "The assistant and faithful companion to The Swordsman."

"Killjoy, can you please pretend for a minute that I don't know anything about all this hocus-pocus mumbo-jumbo and just explain things to me?"

"Ah jeez, where do I begin?"

Killjoy grabs a lamp from Charles' desk and puts it on the floor in the middle of the room. She casts a spell on it, and to Mad's amazement, the lamp begins projecting shadows onto the ceiling that coincide with the story that Killjoy starts to tell.

Chapter 4

The History of The Swordsman, His Squire, and The Night Dwellers.

The shadows projecting on the ceiling unfold the story visibly as Killjoy speaks.

"Contrary to popular belief, this… realm is a lot older than we know, and humans were not its first inhabitants; demons were. For a millennia, monsters ruled the Earth, and humans were nothing more than their pets and cattle. That was until humanity discovered how to harness magic." Shadows of Celtic Druids are seen summoning magic forces at Stonehenge.

"Suddenly, humanity had a legitimate chance to fight their demonic overlords and become the dominant race. The conflict raged on for decades. And then, sometime between the seventh and fifteenth century, Merlin Ambrosius, the greatest sorcerer of them all, assembled the seven most powerful Sorcerers on the planet. They forged the Heavenly Blade with their combined might: a weapon made of pure holy light and capable of slaying even the most powerful of demons. The blade was then bestowed upon one worthy human warrior known only as The Swordsman."

"And thus, with our champion in place, humanity won the war. Most demons were either slain, vanished to the dark realms, or permanently cursed to never step into the sunlight again and only walk the Earth at night. Hence, we refer to the inhuman beings that remained on Earth as Night Dwellers." The shadows of significantly, menacing demons change into more familiar paranormal beings, such as vampires, werewolves, and zombies, on the ceiling.

"To this day, The Swordsman has remained the champion of man; the one that maintains the peace between Humanity and the Night Dwellers. When one Swordsman dies, another worthy warrior takes up the sword and continues his work." The shadow of the Swordsman fades and leaves his sword behind, and a second shadow figure picks up the sword.

"Okay, I dig the epic Peter Jackson prologue," Mad interrupts. "And that thing with the shadows is cool and all, but what does any of this have to do with my dad?"

Killjoy holds up the emblem with the code of arms. "For as long as there has been The Swordsman, there has been The Squire, a pure-hearted faithful companion who stands by humanity's champion, no matter what. This emblem is the code of arms of The Squire. Your dad is honour-bound to serve The Swordsman until the end of his days."

"So, my dad is some monster-fighting, Medieval dude's sidekick?"

"Yeah, basically. The good news is that we now have a lead. If we find The Swordsman, we find your dad—" Killjoy is interrupted by a sudden crash. She sees that Mad has knocked over the display with all of the medieval weapons.

"Why didn't he tell me? Why did he hide all of this from me?" Mad demands.

"Mad, he wanted you to have a normal life without monsters." Killjoy explains. "I mean, can you blame him?"

"I'm going to kill him!"

"What?"

"This Swordsman guy. If something happened to my dad because of him, I swear I'll kill him."

"Okay, fine. We'll kill humanity's only hope against the forces of evil." Killjoy responds, sarcastically. "But we have to find him first."

"How?"

"Easy — all we need to do is figure out what was the last case your dad was working on with The Swordsman before he disappeared. Should be simple enough."

"Right, and we do that how, exactly?"

"We rewind the room."

Madeline stares at her blankly. "You know what, I'm not even going to ask. Just do it, and I'll save my questions for later."

Killjoy stands in the middle of the room and pulls a tiny digital recorder out of her coat pocket.

"Tempo Reversa!"

As she says this, she presses the rewind button on the digital recorder; the displayed numbers on the recorder start to count down to zero at a rapid pace, and to Mad's astonishment, the room quickly changes back to its state before the intruder searched it. Broken items fix themselves, office supplies littering the floor roll back onto tables and their previous location. Soon, the room looks as though it had never been searched.

"Did... did we just time travel?" she asks, in amazement.

"Nah, I just hit a reset button on this room to an hour ago. We are still in the same time. A convenient trick if you knock over someone's wedding cake." She holds up the device. "Just a little something I cooked up. I call it The Rewinder."

"Can you time travel?"

"Focus, Mad!" Killjoy looks around. "There!"

Mad turns to look but sees nothing. "Where?"

"You see the direction of the carpet fibres?"

"Sure."

"That's the last spot your father spent time in this room." Killjoy heads over to the spot and feels around the wall until she finds a hidden compartment there. The compartment is filled with paperwork and manila folders. "This looks promising. Here! These are the last files he handled; I can tell by the—"

"Skip the detective seminar and tell me what's in the file."

Killjoy rolls her eyes and starts going through the papers. "It all looks like information about some kind of high-end auction. Look, he highlighted one item. The Nail of Nefario."

"What's the Nail of Nefario?" Mad asks.

"What the hell do I look like — Wikipedia? I don't know everything!"

"All right, keep your shirt on. Can you tell me what was so important about it?"

"It looks like your dad was trying to trace back the accounts of whoever won this Nail of Nefario at the auction, and yeah, here it is… It was purchased using the accounts of Preston Publications…" Killjoy gets lost in thought when she says the company's name aloud.

"What? Is that bad?" Mad wonders.

"I don't know, but something seems familiar about that name."

Killjoy runs across the room and gets on Charles' computer. She does a web search for Preston Publications, and it quickly takes her to the company's website. She scrolls over the basic information about the company until she sees a button link for the CEO. She clicks on the link, and she is immediately taken to a window with a photo of Light Preston, the owner of the company. Killjoy's eyes widen the moment she sees the image.

Mad runs over and takes a look. "Hey, he's pretty handsome," but she quickly becomes concerned when she sees the blank expression on her companion's face.

"Killjoy, you okay? Is this guy an old boyfriend or something?"

"Or something," Killjoy replies. "You know how I told you that Night Dwellers are not allowed out in the daytime? Meet the monster that stumbled upon a loophole that allows him to live in both. Light Preston is just a disguise. His real name is Loopin Shadows, and he was the first Slasher."

———

Night-time looms over Obscure City. That familiar chill hangs in the air as the clouds turn grey, and the moon glows brighter as it dominates the night sky, with its only rival being the tallest building in the city, Preston Publications; a building so tall it blocks the moonlight and casts an ominous shadow over the streets below.

Inside the colossal edifice is the owner and CEO of this multibillion-dollar corporation, Light Preston. Blessed with wealth and handsome features, the all-powerful businessman stands in his lavish office draped in a twelve hundred-dollar, custom-made suit, and yet he looks displeased by his surroundings as he stares intently into an open vault door on the east wall of his office. The heavy iron door seems to have been cut into several pieces.

Most of the lights in the room are off, allowing Preston to hide his handsome features in shadow.

He is flanked by two strange creatures: Slashers, by definition. The first is Mason Leather, a giant, hulking man with stitches all over his arms and face. The other, Dollface, looks like a four foot-tall living doll, and while he can move his body, his face seems to be frozen in the same creepy expression.

Rip and Torn enter the room with a very apparent look of fear in their eyes.

"Let me see if I understand this correctly," Preston begins. "First, my two deadliest assassins allowed The Swordsman to walk right into my office, cut open my vault and take the Nail of Nefario. I, however, opted to be lenient with you, even though he took the very instrument that will ensure this operation's success. After all, this is the Swordsman we're talking about: he has single-handedly slain Night Dwellers far bigger and more powerful than the two of you combined. But then, I gave you the simple task of kidnapping the Chan girl and bringing her to me." As he continues, he angrily rips off his face revealing it to be a mask. He throws the grotesque human disguise on the floor in front of the two sisters and reveals the hideous features of Loopin Shadows.

"And somehow, someway," Shadows continues, "the two most feared killers in the underworld were thwarted by a Familiar and a Half-Breed who, at the time, had no powers due to being bound in iron!"

Rip and Torn cringe in fear.

Shadows goes from intense rage to eerie calm. "Did I recount all the details correctly?"

"Yes—"

"—Master," they respond.

"Well, then." Shadows holds out his right hand; Mason nervously steps forward and slips a gauntlet with sharp fingertips over his hand.

Rip and Torn's fear is even more apparent now.

Shadows turns around, and while he might be shrouded in darkness, it is still apparent that the handsome businessman is gone, and all that remains is the terrifying Slasher.

"Who wants to assume responsibility for this?" Shadows asks.

The sisters look at each other, but Rip quickly averts her eyes.

Torn takes a deep breath and steps forward. She draws her Sickle Blade and offers it to Shadows.

Shadows smiles. Pointed, shark-like teeth adorn the interior of his mouth. "Excellent, Torn," he says proudly. "You know what to do."

Torn holds her blade up, ready to bring it down on her chest. Rip is visibly distraught by what she is witnessing. Suddenly, Torn turns and throws the blade right at Rip without warning. The metal projectile goes right into her throat. Rip holds the blade with both hands as blood shoots profusely out of her neck.

Torn casually walks over, knocks her hands out of the way, takes the blade, and decapitates her sister with one swift motion.

Rip's headless body hits the ground, creating a large pool of blood around it.

Torn puts Rip's head at Shadows' feet, as she bows to him.

"Atta girl. Mason…?" The ghastly behemoth steps forward, answering his master's call. "Did you find anything in the Chan girl's apartment?"

"No, master." The gargantuan man responds.

"That figures," Shadows says in a disappointed tone. "Take Torn with you and bring the car around. We're due in court in an hour." The two henchmen nod and take their leave.

Shadows looks down at Rip's remains.

"Oh — and Dollface?" he says to his diminutive henchman. "Make sure to tell the janitorial staff that they will need extra hands tonight, and don't forget to apologise for the mess."

Dollface nods and quickly leaves the room.

Chapter 5

A Night in Court

The moon flies higher in the night sky as midnight approaches Obscure City, casting a regal glow on one of the city's oldest and most prestigious structures: the Caligari Cathedral.

Killjoy, Mad, and Hime, mid-conversation, approach the gothic monument.

"So you're saying that those things that attacked me in the alley can just walk around the city in monster form and go unnoticed?" Mad enquires.

"Yeah, this town was originally a sanctuary for Night Dwellers," Killjoy explains. "So when humans started moving in, a Warlock cast a spell on the whole city that makes Night Dwellers unnoticeable to humans."

"But I'm human, and I still noticed them."

"Yeah, but you now know about us, and awareness of the supernatural breaks the spell." Killjoy suddenly remembers something. "By the way, I've been meaning to ask… when you saw me next to the Police Station for the first time, what did I look like?"

"Like Karen Gillan in a pants suit."

"Nice!"

"Okay, then." Mad thinks as she changes the subject. "You're a witch. The two uglies in the alley were Slashers, but what is Hime?"

At that very moment, they look down to see Hime licking himself.

"That is a mystery for another day," Killjoy says, as they all stop in front of the cathedral. "Okay, we're here."

The two find themselves in front of an old statue of a gargoyle.

"Your informant is going to meet us here?" Mad wondered.

"No. This is my informant," Killjoy clarified, pointing at the statue.

"What? This ugly old statue?"

Suddenly the statue comes to life, right before Mad's eyes.

"Hey, who you calling ugly, you little brat?" the Statue barked.

The sudden surprise causes Mad to shriek like a five-year-old and fall right on her butt, as she looks up at a heavy-set, grey statue with a prominent chin, horns, and four-foot wings sticking out of his back.

"Don't know what she's talking about, Stoney," Killjoy interjects. "You're still as handsome as ever."

"Kassandra Killjoy, you little minx." Stoney says, nearly blushing. "Flattery will get you everywhere!"

With this, the gargoyle embraces Killjoy with a friendly hug.

Mad shakes her head and stands up, dusting herself off.

"Madeline Chan," Killjoy begins, "I would like you to meet Granite Stonegast III, King of The Gargoyles."

"Yeah… It's a pleasure," she greets sarcastically. "Killjoy says you can help me find my dad."

"In a hurry, are we?" Stoney says, disapprovingly. "Can't even spare a second to greet royalty properly?"

Mad raises her eyebrows and looks toward Killjoy for support.

Killjoy mouths the words, "Bow, stupid."

Mad quickly follows her instructions and bows to the Gargoyle.

"My… apologies… your Highness," Mad mutters awkwardly.

Killjoy waves her hand, encouraging her to say more.

"I never meant to insult you with my… insubordinate behaviour. You are the best-looking, talking statue I've ever seen."

"All right, all right, don't overdo it. No one likes a suck-up." Stoney motions her to stop as he tries to progress the conversation. "What would you ladies like to know?"

"Stoney, you and your brethren keep a vigilant eye on this city and are aware of the comings and goings of all of its Night Dwellers," Killjoy says.

"Yes, and what of it?"

"We need to know the location of one."

"Kassandra, my dear, you know I am sworn to secrecy unless human lives are in danger."

"I thought you'd say that, and thus we have brought an offering."

Killjoy gestures at Mad to show him the offering they brought. Mad stands there, clueless for a moment, until she finally remembers.

She quickly reaches into her backpack but stops and looks at Killjoy with scepticism. "Killjoy, are you sure about this?"

"Mad, you're making me look bad. Please hurry up."

Mad pulls out a bag of mini marshmallows and offers them to Stoney.

"For you, my... King."

"Oh, those magnificent morsels!" He takes the marshmallows from Madeline and begins pouring them into his mouth. "What do you want to know, my dear?" he asks, munching on the fluffy treats.

"We need to know where Loopin Shadows will be tonight," Killjoy enquires.

Stoney immediately loses his composure and spits marshmallows all over Mad's feet. "Why would either of you want to know the whereabouts of that monster?" Stoney questions with discernible fear in his voice.

"That's our business," Killjoy answers. "Now, we fulfilled our end of the bargain; time for you to fulfil yours."

"Very well, then. The East-Side Clan last saw Shadows and his ilk en route to The Court of Darkness."

"Merciful Malus!" Killjoy exclaims as she takes out her pocket watch to check the time.

"What… What is that?" Mad asks.

"I'll explain when we get there. We need to hurry."

"Ms Chan," Stoney calls, gesturing to get her attention.

"Yes, your Majesty?"

"I do hope you find your father."

Mad is touched for a moment, but Killjoy pulls her away before she gets a chance to thank The Gargoyle King for the sentiment.

As Killjoy, Mad, and Hime head down the street, Stoney transforms back into a statue.

They run at full speed down the wet, unkempt road that leads away from the cathedral. Their footfalls echo off the surrounding buildings as they make their progress.

"Where are we going?" Mad asks, gasping for air.

"The Court of Darkness: it's in the heart of the city, and they're due to meet in less than fifteen minutes," Killjoy replies as she looks at her pocket watch once again.

"You want me to call an Uber?"

"Not fast enough. We're going to have to fly."

"Wait, what?" Mad reacts, nearly tripping on the pavement.

Killjoy pulls her broom out of her coat. It expands to full size in her hand, as she grabs Mad by the back of her shirt, and the thin wooden stick begins to take them into the sky.

"Oh my god! Oh my god! Oh my god!" Mad screams with uncontrollable fear.

Killjoy mounts her broom and swings Mad around her back with one swift motion. She holds on tight, almost reminiscent of a baby chimpanzee clinging to its mother, while Hime jumps inside Mad's backpack with expert precision.

"Hey, Lady, you forgots me," Hime protests.

"Shut up, you stupid cat!" Mad yells, her body trembling as she tightens her grip around Killjoy.

"What's wrong? Never flown on a broom before?" Killjoy playfully teases.

"I hate you!"

They get higher and higher until they are above the skyscrapers.

Killjoy leans forward, and her motion instantly commands her broom to take off in a straight line across the city, on their way to the Court of Darkness, at incredible speed. The buildings turn into blurs as they fly by, and before Mad has a chance to relax, Killjoy slows down and begins her descent.

They land on a rooftop of an old, historical Romanesque courthouse in the city's centre. While the building looks maintained and cared for, its long history is apparent.

Killjoy lands gracefully, like a ballerina, while Mad clumsily stumbles to the ground in desperate grasping for terra firma.

"So the flying broomstick thing is real, huh?" Mad asks, with a notable shake in her voice, trying her best to look calm and collected.

"Yup," Killjoy responds.

"Not a silly Halloween Harry Potter gimmick."

"Nope," Killjoy says, all the while moving towards a skylight. "Now get a hold of yourself, Mad — we have work to do."

They get to the skylight and look inside the building. The glass is yellow and dirty, but the two lie on top of it, pressing their faces against its surface to get a good view. The room is a vast meeting hall with a large stone conference table in the middle. A group of well-dressed individuals begin to enter the room through different doors.

"Oh, good, it's just starting," Killjoy announces.

"What's starting? You haven't explained anything!" Mad protests.

"Okay, you remember how I told you that Merlin gathered seven Sorcerers to create the Heavenly Blade?"

"Yeah."

"Well, shortly after the war, Danapholi, the Demon Queen, selected seven Night Dwellers to represent them in the world of men; the seven most feared and powerful beings in the paranormal world gather as a counsel every month to make the most important decisions."

Killjoy gestures at a giant, red demon in a black suit, about to sit at the stone table. He looks like a stereotypical portrayal of Satan from Christian art and literature.

"That's Demavelos Shard, Duke of Demons."

Next, a tall, mature-looking yet beautiful, raven-haired woman sits next to Demavelos. "She's the Grand Witch, Minerva Madrigal."

An older man with greying hair and a face covered in gruesome surgical scars enters the room. "That's Professor Jaq Pretorious, Reverend of The Re-Animated."

A glistening green, humanoid sea monster joins them. "Gillion DeLongcre, Monarch of the Mariners."

Killjoy sees a familiar figure enter the room, clad in a trench coat with bushy sideburns taking up most of his face. "My good buddy, Kanus Veil, Lord of The Lycans."

Veil is followed into the room by a female mummy still clad in traditional wrappings of ancient Egyptian burial rites, yet adorned in shining gold jewellery and other traditional Egyptian vestments. "That's Loxana Tet, Empress of the Ancients."

Finally, the last member of the court enters. He is a tall, pale, imposing man in a dark Victorian suit. "And last, but not least, the current head of the court: The Vampire King himself, Damian Callus."

Mad watches as the imposing vampire takes his seat at the head of the table.

"Mad Chan, these are the heads of The Seven Families," Killjoy states dramatically

Each member of the court takes their rightful place around the table. Surrounding the room, bodyguards stand with dedicated vigilance.

"So this town is run by seven monster—gangsters?" Mad questions.

"Pretty much," Killjoy confirms.

"That figures."

Killjoy pulls a giant parabolic microphone out of her coat and hands it to Mad.

"Here, take this and point it at them," she instructs.

Mad looks at the device, confused and slightly perplexed.

"Really? No magic?" Mad says in slight surprise.

"Sometimes the human ways are the best ways," Killjoy clarifies. "Plus, at least three individuals down there could detect my magic. Better to be safe than sorry."

Killjoy hands Mad an earbud that's attached to the microphone. They both insert the listening devices into their ears and begin listening in on the mysterious meeting.

Inside the court, Guillion the merman commands the current topic of discussion.

"Twice this week," he begins, "the Kappa Clan has tried to smuggle contraband through my docks, and the Swordsman has yet to do anything about it."

Loxana, the mummy chimes in. "I, too, have noticed that he favours some territories over others."

"Once again, your tiny minds limit your perception," the Professor interjects condescendingly.

Offended, Gullion stands up threateningly.

Damian Callus waves his hand and motions him to sit down. Gullion does so begrudgingly.

"Professor, save your belligerence for your subjects," Callus instructs, "not for your equals. Feel free to enlighten us, though."

"His absence is not due to favouritism," the Professor hypothesises. "Any fool can see that our dear constable has been missing for the past week."

"Typical human," the Demon Demavolus grunts. "I say the time is long overdue for us to be policed by our own kind."

"For once, we agree, Shard," Veil says with enthusiasm. "The humans have their laws and penalties. It's about time we started governing ourselves!"

"We. . ?" a familiar voice echoes through the hall.

Everyone turns their heads to see Loopin Shadows standing at the far side of the room.

He is clad in a brown suit and matching fedora. His features are evident under the lamps of the meeting hall: a malformed, green demon who has part of his face covered by a metal mask. His leathery lips are curled into a sinister smile, containing two rows of shark-like teeth that glisten in the light.

"Isn't that always your cry?" Shadows asks with a hint of mockery. "We, we, we? What about us?" A large gang of Slashers step out of the shadows and surround him as he says this.

Killjoy, Mad, and Hime are still watching from above. Eyebrows furrow as a look of concern overtakes the Paranormal Private-Eye's face.

"Oh no," she mumbles to herself.

"That's him, isn't it?" Mad points at the fedora-wearing demon. "That's Loopin Shadows. That's the guy my dad was investigating!"

"Yeah, but you don't understand. This is bad. I thought Shadows had been asked to appear at the Court of Darkness, but it looks like he's here without an invitation."

"And that's bad because. . ?"

"He's a Slasher. Slashers are greatly discriminated against in the underworld. They are seen as impure, a fusion of a human and a Night Dweller."

"You mean— humans and monsters breeding?" Mad asks with disgust in her tone.

"No, that would be a half-breed like me. Slashers are generally created via an accident or a curse, and the fusion only works on a human with a tainted soul."

"Tainted soul?"

"Serial killers, rapists, psychopaths…" Killjoy explains. "People who were already terrible long before they came into contact with a demon."

Inside, Demavalos Shard angrily stands up and slams his fist on the table.

"You are not worthy of standing in this room, you impure abomination!" he shouts.

"And that's the problem, Mr Shard," Shadows responds with an eerie calm. "According to your standards, I am not worthy of standing anywhere. We are neither human nor Night Dweller, so neither world will ever accept us."

Growing impatient with the turn of events, Callus tries to take control of the situation. "Loopin Shadows! While your extreme rhetoric might be compelling, your presence is not welcomed here. I will ask you only once to leave."

"Damian," Minerva interrupts. "If you don't mind, I would like to hear what Mr Shadows has to say."

Overhead, Killjoy's eyes narrow with curiosity. *What are you up to, Minerva?* she thinks.

"I would also love to hear what the Slasher has to say," Veil says.

"Why? What could he possibly have to say to us?" Guillion questions.

"Are you kidding me? I've been coming to these meetings for a hundred years, and this is the first interesting thing that has ever happened! The man had the balls to walk into a room with the seven most dangerous Night Dwellers in the underworld. I say that at least buys him five minutes of our time."

Everyone but Shard seems to agree to the declaration reluctantly.

"All right then, Mr Shadows," Callus relents. "State your case with great haste, for my patience is wearing thin."

"With gratitude, your Highness," Shadows utters with a wicked smile. "It seems as though this court always has the same two problems: a Swordsman who doesn't represent your best interest and a planet overrun by inferior, weak humans. I can solve both of these problems for you as long as you grant me one small, simple request."

"And what would that be?" Callus asks.

"A seat at your table."

Most of the court laughs, including the bodyguards, who try to keep their chuckles hidden.

"Veil was right," Demavalos admits. "This is the most amusing thing to happen in this court in a long time. You will never sit at this table, you disgusting whelp. Even if we accepted your kind, our laws dictate that only seven representatives may have a chair, and as you can clearly see, all seats are taken."

Shadows nods in agreement, but suddenly, without warning, he holds out his gauntlet and fires a long sharp fingernail directly at Shard.

The nail hits Shard square in the chest, and before he has time to react, he is consumed by a fireball of white and black flame. When the flame dies down, all that remains of Demavalos Shard is a pile of ash and bone.

Shadows laughs, completely satisfied with his work. "Well, it seems like you now have a vacancy. Problem solved."

Everyone is stunned and shaken by Shadows' action and they sit in complete shock while Shadows walks over to the table. He brushes off what's left of Demavalos Shard and takes a seat.

His entourage of Slashers protectively stand around him.

The Professor's curiosity gets the better of him as he breaks the silence. "What was in that projectile, boy?"

"The two most volatile elements in our world: pure light and pure darkness," Shadows explains. "I have high explosives at my fingertips. Literally. Hopefully, I won't forget, go to pick my nose, and blow my own head off."

Veil laughs loudly and with gusto. The rest of the group looks at him with disapproval.

"What? It was funny," he says, struggling to regain his composure.

Having seen enough, Killjoy is satisfied with their surveillance, "Okay. We have a Slasher with a weapon of mass destruction strapped to his arm, claiming he can overthrow humanity. We need to find The Swordsman now!"

Suddenly, Killjoy and Mad hear a faint cracking sound followed by what seems to be splintering wood.

"What was that?" Mad asks, highly concerned.

Looking down, Killjoy notices a crack in the skylight they are occupying. She tries to yell at Mad to get off the glass, but before Killjoy can say anything, the skylight that they are lying on cracks and shatters, bringing both of them careening down into the Court.

The seven Night Dwellers and their bodyguards have no time to react as Killjoy and Mad fall out of the sky and crash through the stone table the seven are occupying.

Hime follows and lands gracefully on his paws, licking himself as if nothing happened. "I gotta fix my hairs."

Surprised, the occupants of the Court stand up and back away with weapons and bodyguards at the ready. However, when the dust and debris from the collapse dissipate, they see the awkwardly dressed Witch Detective and a very petite, teenaged human, looking worse for wear.

"Now I know what Mick Foley feels like," Killjoy mutters to herself, trying to pick herself up to get to her feet.

"Killjoy!" Callus exclaims.

"Oh, great!" Veil grumbles.

Minerva, however, seems to be the angriest in the group. "What are you doing here, Kassandra?" she yells.

"Nice to see you too, Minerva!" Killjoy responds sarcastically. "Would any of you know where the In 'n' Out Burger is on this block? There's something wrong with our GPS."

Professor Pretorius draws out a cattle prod, slowly inching his way closer to them.

Killjoy quickly summons her broom. It flies into her hand, and she points the end of it at the Professor, holding it like an assault rifle.

All the Night Dwellers take a step back.

"Not so fast, old man," Killjoy says confidently. "Just because you have us surrounded, outnumbered, and outmatched doesn't mean we won't go down fighting."

Hime jumps in front of Killjoy and Mad and growls at the Night Dwellers, inadvertently looking pretty adorable in his attempt to intimidate.

Mad, meanwhile, grabs a piece of wood from the broken skylight, holding it in her outstretched hand, awkwardly, as a makeshift weapon.

Minerva grows even more frustrated now. "Kassandra, don't do anything foolish."

"Hey, thanks for the suggestion, Minerva," Killjoy replies, with much sarcasm.

Suddenly Mad notices Shadows' giant henchman, Mason Leather. "Hey, Killjoy. Look at that guy. Seven feet tall, dumb-looking. That's the guy who broke into my apartment!" The gargantuan man smiles sheepishly.

Killjoy rolls her eyes. "Mad, as impressed as I am with your powers of deduction, this is not the time!"

Damian Callus tries to regain control of the room. "Ms Killjoy, I—"

Suddenly, Hime interrupts. "Hey deh Stinky Feets, these are my persons. They belong to me," he growls.

"Bloody hell, that cat can talk!" Veil exclaims.

"I've got to get better sidekicks," Killjoy grumbles.

"Sidekicks?" Mad protests.

"Enough!" Callus shouts while, once again, trying to re-establish his authority. "My patience has expired, Witch. So much so that if one of my associates desires to kill you and your companions, I feel inclined to let them do it."

"Plenty of volunteers in this room," Vail gleefully exclaims.

The Night Dwellers brandish their weapons as they move in on the three intruders.

"Not so fast!" Killjoy shouts as she points her broomstick right at Shadows' gauntlet. "One plasma bolt at Mr. Smiley's explody glove, and we all go up together."

Shadows smirks, seemingly very amused by this threat. "Oh, I am starting to like you."

Realizing that Killjoy is right, the Night Dwellers lower their weapons.

"That's right; you better back up," Killjoy says.

Suddenly, Mad taps Killjoy on the shoulder. "Not now, Mad; we got them on the ropes," she whispers, not wanting to let her guard down.

"Not that, Killjoy — look!" Mad is pointing at something behind her. Killjoy sees The Swordsman perched on the windowsill behind her when she turns around.

He is a tall, dashing figure wearing a long coat that seems to bellow heroically in the wind. An old bowler hat adorns the top of his head, but it is tipped forward, so the brim hides half the features of his face.

The Swordsman reaches just over his right shoulder where the Heavenly Blade can be seen sheathed at his back. The moment his hand wraps around the blade's handle, The Night Dwellers ignore Killjoy, Mad, and Hime, turning all their attention and weapons to The Swordsman.

Taking the hint, Killjoy whispers to Mad and Hime. "That's our cue!" The three of them leave the room as quickly as they can, while The Night Dwellers' gaze remains on The Swordsman.

Once the three are safe, the mysterious hero lets go of the blade, diving out of the window behind him, vanishing into the night.

The Night Dwellers are stunned; left humiliated in their meeting hall with nothing to show for it besides a broken table, broken ceiling, and the ashy remains of their former comrade.

"Mr Shadows… we accept your offer," Callus says, his gaze not leaving the spot where The Swordsman once stood. "If you can do away with The Swordsman and give us the leverage we need against the humans, we will put aside our prejudice and give you a seat at our table. Does anyone oppose?" Some of the court members are visibly taken aback by his words, yet no one dares speak a word.

"Thank you, Your Highness. If you don't mind, I have a Swordsman to hunt," Shadows says. He gives an exaggerated bow and then motions for his fellow Slashers to follow him. Together, they leave the Court of Darkness.

"Damian, you cannot be serious! Allowing that repulsive anomaly to have a seat of honour at our Court?" Loxana yells, her shrill voice betraying her calm composure.

"Loxana, my dear, what do we have to lose?" Callus reassures her. "If he fails, The Swordsman will kill him. Yet if he succeeds…" Callus picks up one of Shard's bones, examining it in his hands, "The Demon clan will destroy him as revenge for killing their master and taking his seat. Either way, we win."

"Shadows is no fool," Minerva offers. "He wouldn't have made such a bargain if he didn't have a plan."

"Let him try. It's all of us against a handful them. At the end of the night, they are still just a minority."

Outside the Court of Shadows, Killjoy, Mad, and Hime run out of the old building, stopping to catch their breath in the middle of the empty street, once they feel they are at a safe distance.

"We fell — like — fifty feet!" Mad exclaims, still trying to catch her breath. "How are we not crippled or … dead?"

"I cushioned our fall at the last second," Killjoy says, "but we still technically fell at full speed for about five feet and destroyed a table with our bodies. We might want to stop on the way home and pick up some Icy Hot."

Suddenly, Mad spots a dark figure sliding down the fire escape on the side of a nearby building, and landing in the alleyway next to it. It's The Swordsman!

"Hey, you!" Mad shouts.

Surprised, Killjoy and Hime turn to look at The Swordsman.

"You know where my father is!" Mad shouts as she pulls her skateboard out of her backpack and begins to chase after the mystery man.

At the sound of Mad's voice, The Swordsman turns and runs down the road.

Mad, desperate to catch The Swordsman, displays her impressive skateboarding skills as she gets closer and closer to the legendary warrior, almost touching his billowing coat with her fingertips.

Just as she is about to rap her fingers around a portion of the coat and catch him, one of the wheels on her skateboard suddenly falls off, causing Mad to wipe out on the sidewalk, scraping her hands and knee in the process.

She looks up just in time to see The Swordsman jump into a convertible and drive away.

Killjoy flies down on her broom and lands next to Mad while Hime teleports right by her injured leg. He sweetly rubs his little body against her leg.

"Mad, why did you take off like that?" Killjoy questions. "I could have flown you. We could have caught him."

"Sorry, okay? I just… I feel so damned useless," Mad laments, tears travelling down her freckled cheeks. "I wanted to do something— something on my own to find my dad."

"It's okay, Mad. We'll find him, I promise. Now, let me see your knee." Killjoy reaches into her coat pocket, procuring a fully stocked first-aid kit. While Killjoy tends to the injury, Mad wipes away her tears, attempting to compose herself.

"So… you're a half-breed?" Mad asks.

"Yup."

"Which means one of your parents is human and the other—"

"—is not."

"Are your parents cool?"

"It depends on your definition of cool. My dad is your stereotypical, brave, human idiot, and my mom… well, that's a long story."

"Did they love each other?"

"Yeah. When they first met, they did. But then something came along that reminded them just how different they were."

"What was that?"

"Me."

Killjoy finishes bandaging Mad's knee and helps her to her feet. "There you go. Good as new. Now let's get you home. It's been a long night, and you have school tomorrow."

"What? You expect me to go to school while we're in the middle of all this?" Mad protests.

"Yup. There's nothing we can do until tomorrow night when all the creatures come out."

"*Argh*! I have to go through a whole school day with maybe one hour of sleep? This is going to suck," Mad grumbles.

"Oh, don't worry! I can compress your sleep so you can get eight hours of rest in just a few minutes," Killjoy smiles, while they both start the journey back to Mad's apartment.

"Okay, out of all your magic tricks, that's my favourite so far."

Chapter 6

The Nail of Nefario and its Nefarious Applications

The rising sun that casts its light over Obscure City in the early mornings somehow hides the city's true identity as its citizens go about their day.

The Number 48 District School Bus zooms past traffic in its designated lane to Ray Harryhausen High School. Mad sits on the very back seat of the bus writing in her notebook.

Dear diary… I wish I could tell you that I've found my dad, and things are back to normal, but normal is a state I will never be in ever again. Discovering my dad's world has changed my perspective on everything and made my life seem much smaller.

The bus driver stops to let a few kids in and closes the door behind them. Mad notices there is a rosary on the inside of the bus door with a cross attached to it. She looks back at the bus driver, who has seen her looking at the cross. The driver smiles at her, nods, and continues driving.

Time progresses throughout her school day as usual, but Mad notices more evidence of the paranormal: pale, Goth kids who stick to the shadows and avoid the sunlight shining through the windows at all costs. She also notices how the leader of the popular girls has a voodoo charm on her bracelet, and she seems to almost be controlling the other popular girls with simple hand gestures. She turns away from the Goths and the popular girls just in time to see one of the swim-team members trying to hide the gills on his neck under his long hair.

I feel like I spent all my life with my eyes closed until Killjoy came along. It's like she taught me how to open them and see what has been in front of me all along.

Before classes are set to begin, Mad stops by the library. She picks out books about Ancient Greek and Egyptian Mythology and anything she can find regarding vampires, werewolves and the supernatural.

My dad always says, 'Luck favours the prepared.' Well, I'm sick of being unprepared. If the monsters that come out at night took him, I'm going to be ready for them.

The day goes by slowly. Mad distracts herself by hiding the books she checked out of the library within her textbooks and reading them during class.

Truth is: I've never fitted in anywhere. There's not a single group in school that I can honestly say I belong to. But last night, running around town with Killjoy, even though I was in more danger than I've ever been in my life, it felt... right somehow. If I survive all of this, I think I might ask Killjoy for a job as her assistant, or Junior

Detective, or something. Cause I really can't picture myself having a regular job, or life, after this.

Minute by minute, hour by hour, the day continues to pass. While the rest of her classmates enjoy their lunch period, eating and hanging out with friends, Mad spends the hour in the metal-shop classroom, fixing her skateboard and making crude weapons, like wooden stakes, a simple silver knife, and what could pass off as brass knuckles with iron rivets. They are crude, and hastily put together with what little time she has, but they'll do.

I'm sorry, dad. I'm not like you. I could never be content being an accountant or just a sidekick; I have to take matters into my own hands. I will find you. Wherever you are, I will find you and every Night Dweller that gets in my way better watch out 'cause tonight, I'm ready for them.

As the sun sets on the supernatural city, a public transit bus makes its routine stop in front of Killjoy Komics. Mad exits the bus, where Hime greets her.

"Hey Lady, you gots any snacks for my mouff?"

"You bet I do, buddy," Mad answers, as she kneels and offers Hime little pieces of a hotdog in a Ziploc bag she procures from her backpack.

Hime scarfs them down, while making his usual comical sound, "Yum, Yum, Yum." Satisfied with his snack, Killjoy's familiar leads Mad into the comic book store.

Unknown to her, a familiar figure watches her from the rooftop of a nearby building. The Swordsman's eyes never leave their charge.

Mad enters the comic book store and looks around. She spots the only employee, Dan The-Comic-Book-Man, and strides up confidently.

"Hello, I'm looking for Kassandra Killjoy."

Looking up, Dan's eyes widen with wonder. "Woah, the Squire's daughter," he responds with awe. "Pleasure to meet you, bro. I'm Dan, Dan The-Comic-Book-Man." He raises a fist as an open invitation for a fist bump. Mad awkwardly raises her fist and reciprocates.

"Um, yeah, nice to meet you, too. Killjoy. . ?"

"Boss Lady is in the back, in her office. It looks like a bathroom, but — like — it's not, and yet it is."

Mad stares at him with growing confusion. "Um… Thanks."

She heads to the back, where Dan gestures and enters Killjoy's bathroom/office as Hime follows. After what she's been through, an office disguised as a bathroom doesn't seem so odd.

Killjoy stands at the opposite side of the room, with her back turned to Mad, as she looks over a massive wall covered in evidence, photographs, and clues from the case. Hime runs across the room, climbing a cat tree, and begins licking himself, after declaring, "I gotta fix my hairs."

The Witch Detective looks worse for wear as Mad walks closer. She is barefoot, clad in a pair of Doopy the Delightful Dragon pyjamas, her hair a giant, red, tangled mess, and her eyes have the beginnings of dark circles underneath them. It's evident that Killjoy never went to bed and stayed up all day studying the case.

Mad is in no way disturbed by Killjoy's appearance as she, instead, finds herself in awe of The Witch's office. There are incredible items just sitting and collecting dust almost everywhere she looks. Her state of wonder is only broken when she notices Killjoy's cluttered evidence wall.

"You've been busy," Mad observes.

"Couldn't sleep," Killjoy responds, eyes never leaving the board. "A question kept me up all day."

"What question?"

"Why did he run?"

"Who?"

"The Swordsman."

Mad is surprised she didn't think about that herself. "Damn, you're right. If the guy is such a badass monster killer, why did he run from a tiny Chinese girl on a skateboard?"

"Exactly," Killjoy grunted. "This case just has too many unanswered questions. What is Loopin Shadows' true agenda? What the hell is the Nail of Nefario? Hell, I don't even know who Nefario is!"

"He was a fifteenth-century Wizard," Mad answers, much to Killjoy's surprise.

Turning around, Killjoy looks at Mad with a mixture of shock and curiosity.

"Wait, how did you know that?"

"I Googled it."

Mad reaches into her backpack and pulls out a stack of papers she printed out from her school library.

Flabbergasted, Killjoy snatches the papers out of her hand. "I spent all day pouring over the chronicles. All. Day." She points at a big stack of books on her desk. "And it was on the internet all along?"

"Sometimes, the human ways are the best ways," Mad says, with a smirk and a sly tone.

Killjoy shakes her head and goes over the printouts she arranged on her messy desk. "Okay, smarty. Anything in here about The Nail of Nefario?"

"Nah. Every website I looked at said the same thing. Nefario was an evil douchebag. So a lot, and I mean a lot, of people tried to kill him."

Killjoy's eyes land on one of the pages. Her lips curl into a smile, letting out a small chuckle. "And it just so happens that I know one of them." She turns the page around, pointing at a picture and showing it to Mad.

The picture is of an old, stained-glass window, similar to ones you would find in a catholic church or a medieval castle. The window has a portrait of two people: one is a knight, and the other is who Mad assumes to be Nefario. Both look to be in some type of battle.

"You see the knight that Nefario is fighting in this picture?" Killjoy asked.

"Yeah."

"That is Sir Kadovan Killjoy. My dad!"

"Cool, I…" Mad's eyes widen as a sudden realisation comes over her face. "Wait, your dad was a medieval knight?"

"Yep!"

"Killjoy — when exactly were you born?" Mad asks with equal curiosity and confusion.

"Towards the end of the Crusades," she answers.

"But that would mean you're over seven hundred years old!" Mad squeals.

"Yes, but I don't look a day over three hundred! Isn't that crazy?"

"Holy hell!" Mad whispers, falling back into a chair. Her knees feel weak with the unexpected, shocking information.

Killjoy suddenly heads for the door, motioning for Mad to follow. "Come on — we have a lead."

Mad sits there, staring at her with a questioning look.

"What?" Killjoy asked.

"Um… Are you sure you don't want to change out of your Doopy The Delightful Dragon pyjamas before fighting the forces of evil?"

"Oh, right. Probably a good idea." With a quick hand gesture, Killjoy's pyjamas change into her trademark suit and blue coat. She smooths and straightens her tie as the messy bush of red hair atop her head grooms itself and then contorts into the two waist-long braids she usually wears. She grabs her broom from the hooks on the wall and her wide-brimmed hat from the hat rack, and checks her pocket watch.

"Come along, Mad, Hime — we have work to do."

Mad shakes off the amazement from what she just witnessed. "Where are we going?"

"We're going to ask my dad about the Nail of Nefario."

"Wait — he's still alive?"

"Well… Not exactly."

The sun has set and darkness begins to creep over the city once more. The Obscure City Cemetery takes on a sinister appearance in the moonlight, yet Killjoy and Mad make their way through the tombstones, using flashlights to cut through the encroaching blackness. Hime follows along, showing no sign of worry.

"So, are you immortal?" Mad finally breaks the silence.

"No, witches die all the time," Killjoy responds, slightly annoyed. "Haven't they taught you about the Salem Witch Trials at your school?"

"Yeah, but we're taught they were innocent women who were killed, not actual Witches," Madeline explains. "I still can't believe it. Seven hundred years old, and you look like you're only thirty!"

"We age differently. We age slowly in our first hundred years, and then we stop aging when we reach adulthood. Same goes for most Night Dwellers."

"That's insane!"

"What's really insane is how much humans achieve in their ridiculously short lifespans," Killjoy says. "Most three hundred-year-old Warlocks I know are still living in their parents' basements."

Their conversation is interrupted by a sudden, low rumbling noise which takes them both by surprise, stopping them dead in their tracks.

"What was that?" Mad asks, with fear in her voice.

"Oh no… I was afraid of this."

"Afraid of what?"

"Early Risers."

Mad wants to ask what Early Risers are but she has a feeling she's going to find out. Her eyes dart around the graveyard, searching.

Out of the corner of her eye, she notices the ground twitch and move. Her eyes widen as five different graves burst at the same time, sending wood and earth in every direction. When the debris clears, Killjoy, Mad, and Hime find themselves surrounded by very feral-looking vampires.

Noticing the trouble brewing, Killjoy draws her broom, holding it like a shotgun, ready to fight at a moment's notice.

Hime lowers his head and growls, "Hey deh stinky feets! These are my persons! They belong to me!"

Mad pulls out the wooden stake she made earlier that day, holding it like a spear close to her shoulder; her body taking up a crude fighting stance.

"Where did you get that?" Killjoy asks.

"I made it at school." Mad looks pretty proud of this, and it shows in her voice.

Killjoy is slightly impressed and reaches into her coat pocket and pulls out a medium-sized wooden mallet.

"Here, take this."

Mad is taken aback but grabs the mallet anyway, still trying to keep an eye on the advancing vampires. "What for? I have a weapon already."

"Do you know how hard it is to drive a wooden stake through a rib cage?" Killjoy explains. "You need Slayer strength for that."

"What's a Slayer?" Mad asks.

"A show you need to watch if you want to continue being friends."

The Vampire suddenly jolts and pounces towards them before they can continue their conversation.

Acting quickly, Killjoy knocks away three of them close to Mad with a plasma bolt from her broom. Hime, meanwhile, diverts two of them with his teleportation powers, tricking them and causing both to crash through a tombstone.

"What's wrong with these things? They're so mindless!" Mad yells, while swinging her mallet at a few making their way towards her.

"These are not purebloods — they were turned. Only natural-born vampires are the smooth, sexy Ann Rice type," Killjoy explains. "When a Vampire turns a human, this is what we get. Big, dumb, hungry, feral vamps."

One vamp jumps at Mad, but she kicks him back and follows up her attack by stabbing him in the chest with her homemade stake, but just as Killjoy warned, the stake gets stuck in his rib cage and fails to kill him. "Damn it!"

"I told you!" Killjoy yells.

"Shut up!" Mad shouts as she whacks the Vamp across the face with the wooden mallet. It does nothing, as the rabid creature keeps advancing and attacking. Mad pulls out a second stake from her bag, for round two. Before they can tussle one more time, a large net comes out of the darkness, entangling the Vamp and leaving it incapacitated. The beast growls and hisses as it fails to escape its bonds.

Surprised at the sudden turn of events, Mad looks around to see all the other vampires dealing with the same predicament. Nets have them captured, and they all struggle pointlessly to escape.

Only one vampire is left standing. It turns around and tries to run for it. It doesn't get far. After the vamp takes a few steps, someone jumps out of the shadows and stabs it with a cattle prod, electrocuting it. When the vampire hits the ground, it foams at the mouth, shaking pathetically.

"You girls better take your Halloween party elsewhere," the mystery man wielding the cattle prod instructs. "The cemetery is a suck-head zone tonight."

Killjoy narrows her eyes as a sense of familiarity hits her. "Gar?"

The man steps closer, allowing Killjoy and Mad to finally get a good look at their saviour.

Killjoy's eyes widen as realization and pure joy takes over her complexion. "Ha ha! Mad, this is my old pal Garrett Kayhill!"

Garret Kayhill is a very rugged-looking, blue-collar man. He is dressed in dirty, common work boots and a dark blue jumpsuit. He's a well-fit man with a barrel chest and a chiselled, lantern jaw complete with a permanent five-o'clock shadow.

"Kassandra Killjoy?" Garret sounds equally surprised and just as pleased to see the Witch. "Come here, you sultry sorceress."

Making their way towards each other, they embrace. Garret gives Killjoy a hearty bear hug and a very enthusiastic kiss to the cheek. She blushes and playfully puts her hand on his chest. "Merciful Malus! It's good to see you! I see you're still hitting the gym, too," she says, with a smirk.

"Yeah, just trying to keep in shape," Garret says modestly. "Chasing Vamps is a young man's game, and I'm no spring chicken. Hey, how about you? You're still prettier than a brand new Trans-Am!"

Killjoy giggles and blushes at the compliment, while twiddling one of her braids in her fingers. "Oh, stop!"

"No, seriously, stop!" Mad groans. "Any more old-people flirting, and I will throw up on the cat."

Hime growls a low warning at this.

Killjoy is knocked out of her stupor by the sound of Mad's voice. She seems to have forgotten that her companions even exist. "Oh, geez, I'm sorry. Where are my manners? Gar, this is my new familiar, Hime."

"Hey deh mistah, these are my persons," Hime explains.

"Ah, new blood!" Garret smiles and waves at the Hime while putting his arm around Killjoy's shoulders. "Watch out for this one; she's as beautiful as she is dangerous." Killjoy giggles at this so hard she accidentally lets out a loud snort.

Mad rolls her eyes at the display.

"Oh, this is my new client and bestie, Mad Chan," Killjoy clarifies.

"A pleasure, Miss Chan," Garret smiles. "Garrett Kayhill, VampEx, at your service all night and every night."

"VampEx?" Mad asks.

Garret pulls a business card out of his pocket, handing it to Mad. Taking the card, she examines it closely. It reads 'Garrett Kayhill VampEx - Vampire Exterminations 1-800-VAMPEXX.'

"You're a vampire exterminator?" Mad exclaims, in utter surprise.

"Yup! And you thought your job sucked," Garret says with too much enthusiasm. Both Garret and Killjoy laugh at his joke a little too enthusiastically.

Mad rolls her eyes at their needlessly extreme cackling.

Noticing Mad's annoyance, Garret's laughing slows down and he clears his throat. "Sorry — a little vampire exterminator humour."

"So, Gar — not that I'm complaining, but what are you doing here?" Killjoy asks. "Hitting newborn Vamps at the source?"

"No, nothing that proactive. The folks who own this cemetery have me on retainer. I hit this place twice a week and today just so happened to be one of those days. How about you? Why are you out here playing Scooby-Doo with Velma over here?"

"Velma?" Mad protests.

"We're here to talk to my dad," Killjoy explains, ignoring Mad's exasperation.

"Kadovan? Oh, sweetie, you're on the wrong path. The mausoleums are that way," Garrett explains, while pointing behind them in the opposite direction to where they were travelling.

"Damn it! Every time they expand this place, they make it more confusing."

"Not as confusing as you not returning any of my calls."

"I get busy."

"I liked to get busy."

"Okay!" Mad loudly interjects. "We have a case to solve. So thank you for the directions and the Vamp… Exing, Garrett, but we've got to get going." Mad starts pulling Killjoy away from Garrett by the arm, dragging her in the direction of the mausoleums.

Garrett laughs as the small teenager awkwardly manhandles Killjoy. "Hey, Killjoy!" Garret calls out. "You need anything, you give old Gar a call! You understand?"

"You got it, Gar. We'll talk later." Killjoy stumbles clumsily as Mad pulls her away down the shadowy path.

Garrett chuckles as he begins rounding up his captured vampires, while watching their retreating forms.

The north-east quarter of the cemetery is one of its oldest sections, featuring plots that date back to the 1800s. Killjoy leads the way with her flashlight, as Mad and Hime follow.

"I don't get you," Mad rants. "You face off against monsters and vampires like you're Xena Warrior Princess, but you run into the Brawny Man, and you turn into one of the giggling girls from my school."

"Physical attraction is a natural response all beings have, Mad," Killjoy lectures. "Remind me to make fun of you next time you run into the person that makes you giggle like a schoolgirl."

"Ha! Don't hold your breath."

"Hold that thought. We're here," Killjoy says as she comes to a stop in front of an old concrete structure with a sign over the entryway that reads 'Mausoleo Autem Heroibus' — Latin for Mausoleum of Heroes.

The Witch, Human, and Cat slowly enter the heroic shrine as Killjoy further exposits. "Towards the end of his life, my father went on a few missions for The Holy

Alliance, so when he passed away, they brought his body here to The Mausoleum of Heroes. Originally, I moved to this town to be closer to him, but I ended up settling down."

"You still haven't explained how we'll talk to your dead father," Mad reminds.

"With this." Killjoy holds out a small vial of water.

"What is that? Holy Water?"

"Close. These are the tears of children."

Mad is slightly disturbed. "I don't even want to know how you got those."

"Yeah, that was a long week at the day-care. Anyway, children and some animals are tuned to the part of the visual spectrum in which Ghosts are visible. That's why they're the first to perceive a spectral entity when a house is haunted. Generally, the child believes the entity to be an imaginary friend."

"Wait," Mad interrupts in utter shock. "So you're saying that every time a little kid has an imaginary friend, it's a ghost?"

"Pretty much."

"Mr Bobo was a ghost? God, that's freaking creepy! Congratulations, Killjoy — you just ruined my childhood."

"You're welcome. Anyway, you pour some child tears right into your eyes, and you'll be able to see ghosts again."

"Fine. Just hand over the bottle, and let's get this over with."

"Woah, Mad. Hold your horses. That's a bad idea."

"Why?"

"You'll be able to see every ghost everywhere. It can be very disturbing. Most humans can't handle it. Plus, I'm not sure how long it will be before it wears off. It could be an hour; it might be more."

"Killjoy, I need to find my dad, and if seeing ghosts gets me closer to finding him, I'm doing it."

Killjoy hesitates for a moment. "All right. Can't say I didn't warn you."

Killjoy unscrews the bottle of child tears revealing the cap to have a water dropper attached to it.

"Tilt your head back, and don't blink," Killjoy instructs.

Mad does as the Witch says, with little hesitation. Killjoy carefully pours a single drop of child tears into each of Mad's eyes.

Instantly, Mad feels a weird sensation in her eyes, like when her vision adjusts after going out in the bright sunlight after being in a dark room.

She can see Killjoy performing the same operation on her own eyes, and then suddenly, the ghosts start to come into focus.

About a dozen spectres inhabit the mausoleum. They are all silvery-white and translucent.

Mad looks out of the mausoleum doorway and sees that hundreds of ghosts populate the cemetery. Some seem as pristine as a living person, while others bear the damage from the cause of their death.

Killjoy approaches her companion with the utmost concern. "You okay, Mad?"

"There's… a lot of kids."

"Yeah. The world is a pretty messed-up place."

"Let's get this over with."

Our heroes approach the resting place of Sir Kadovan Killjoy. It is a beautiful marble casket with the likeness of Sir Killjoy adorning the lid and sides.

"Hola Papá. It's me," Killjoy greets. "I need to ask you some questions, if you have a minute."

A few seconds go by, and nothing happens.

"Does it usually take this long?" Mad wonders.

"He likes to make an entrance."

Right on cue, Sir Kadovan Killjoy grandly appears before them, like a magician reappearing after a trick.

"Ay, Mi Linda Querida," Sir Kadovan begins. "You look as beautiful as your mother."

"Holy Hecate, don't say that!" Killjoy demands.

Killjoy and her father go to touch hands, and even though part of her hand goes right through his, they continue the gesture of affection as if it were an everyday occurrence.

"Papá, this is my new client and friend, Mad Chan."

Sir Kadovan greets her in a very formal fashion, complete with a bow, and proceeds to introduce himself in the most elaborate of fashions.

"Sir Kassious Kadovan Killjoy at your service, madam. Knight of the Realm, The Spear of Spain, and proud representative of The Holy Alliance."

"Yeah, I'm Madeline Chan," Mad responds awkwardly, "but Killjoy calls me Mad… for some reason."

"My dear daughter does have her peculiar habits."

"Tell me about it," Mad agrees.

"All right, enough about me!" Killjoy interrupts, "Papá, we need your help."

Killjoy pulls out the piece of paper with the stained-glass picture depicting the battle between him and Nefario. "We need to know about this."

"Ah, Nefario — that demented delinquent. We had many battles."

"Did any of those battles involve something called the Nail of Nefario?"

"They still call it that?" the knight exclaims, rather pleased with himself. "Ha, I gave it that name myself!"

"Cool."

Killjoy goes to high-five her father, but once again, her hand just goes right through his.

"Yes, young lady, one of our encounters did involve the Nail," he continues. "It was our final encounter. Why do you ask?"

"I believe Mad's father took the Nail from a local gangster."

"What? Really?" Mad interjects.

"Why do you think they ambushed you in the alley and searched your place?" Killjoy clarifies. "They were looking for the Nail. Your father and The Swordsman must have stolen it from Shadows after winning it at the auction.

He must know that your dad was The Squire and was so desperate to get the Nail back that he came after you directly.”

“Fat load of good it would have done him,” Mad comments. “I didn’t know anything about this stuff until yesterday.”

Killjoy nods in agreement as she turns her attention back towards her father. “Which brings me to my next question, Papá. If Shadows wants this thing so badly that he is willing to risk exposing his kind in broad daylight, it must be pretty damned important. So, what does the Nail of Nefario do?”

“Throughout his years of villainy,” the Knight explains, “Nefario only had a few Night Dwellers doing his bidding. He created the Nail to expand his ranks.”

“What?” Mad asks.

“If a Night Dweller inserts the Nail of Nefario into his heart, the Nail emits a blinding light that gives all surrounding humans aspects of that creature and transforms them into Night Dwellers.”

“Holy Hecate — an instant army!” Killjoy exclaims.

“Exactly. Nefario was going to build an army of Night Dwellers, and any time he lost soldiers, he could easily replace them using his enemies’ troops.”

“Night Dwellers would no longer be a minority,” Killjoy concludes.

“Thankfully, the Holy Alliance and I stopped him and hid the Nail. Which makes it quite vexing how that demonic device was simply bought at an auction!" he adds, with great displeasure.

"Yeah, that's pretty lame," Killjoy agrees.

As they talk, Mad sees the Swordsman watching them from the mausoleum entrance. She casually grabs her skateboard and then throws it at him.

The skateboard hits the Swordsman right in the face, so hard that one of its wheels falls off and rolls away.

The mysterious warrior falls to the ground in a very undignified manner. Before he can attempt to make a run for it. Mad jumps on him and wrestles him to the ground.

Killjoy turns just in time to see Mad pounce on him.

"Can't say she doesn't learn."

Killjoy goes running after Mad when her father's words stop her.

"Kassandra, mi amor," he warns. "Please be careful; that young lady is in more danger than she knows."

"I will, Papá." With this, Killjoy takes off after her friend.

"Vaya con Dios, mi querida," Sir Kadovan proclaims as he vanishes.

Outside the mausoleum, the Swordsman struggles with Mad and eventually evades her grasp and gets away. He staggers to his feet and clumsily tries to run, but suddenly a chain wraps itself around his ankles and he falls right on his face, losing his hat.

Mad turns to see Killjoy holding the other end of the chain, which is her magic pocket watch.

"Yeah, yeah, I know you're in a hurry," the Witch says in a cocky tone. "But we need to chat."

Killjoy effortlessly drags him across the grass and picks him up by the shirt, ready to play bad cop, when she suddenly recognises the man before her.

"Cal?"

Mad quickly gets closer to better look at the man in Killjoy's grasp.

"Sergeant Calhoun!"

The man behind the front desk at the Obscure Police Department is the one who has been posing as The Swordsman.

Killjoy drops him on the ground and points her broom at him. Mad pulls out her makeshift silver knife. Killjoy is shocked by her weapon, but keeps her focus on Calhoun.

"Where's my dad?" Mad demands.

"And why are you dressed as The Swordsman?" Killjoy adds.

"How do you know I'm not the Swordsman?" Calhoun questions with a slight crack in his voice.

Mad loses her patience and puts her knife to his throat.

"Okay, okay… Jesus!" Calhoun cries out. "Look, I don't know where your old man is. He hired me to dress up like this and pretend to be The Swordsman."

"Why?" Killjoy asks.

"He said he needed a decoy: someone to pretend to be The Swordsman so he and the real Swordsman could have regular lives. He would send me an envelope with money and a location. I would put on the costume, stand on a rooftop, the monsters would take one look at me and scatter. Easy money."

"That's it?" Killjoy responded with scepticism in her voice. "You put on a costume and play pretend? Not good enough, Cal. There's something bigger at play here. You got to give me something more."

"Like I said, I don't know where Charles is," Calhoun reassures her. "But I know where he might be."

Chapter 7

Secrets of The Swordsman

Just a few blocks from the residential area of Obscure lies the abandoned business district. What was once a booming cavalcade of activity is now an empty monument of decay. Calhoun drives our heroes to a defunct Fortune Cookie factory in his old, beaten-up convertible.

Killjoy, Mad, and Hime follow Calhoun into the building. Killjoy keeps her broom trained on him, unwilling to give him a shred of trust.

"Every great now and then, Charles would meet me here whenever he owed me money or gave me this costume," Calhoun explains. "He owes me a little extra scratch since I made my cameo appearance at The Court of Darkness. He said he'd give me a bonus after the fact to cover the added danger of making an appearance in a room with the seven most powerful monsters on the face of the Earth."

"Yeah, really brave," Mad says sarcastically. "I loved how you ran from a high schooler on a skateboard."

"Hey, the lump on the back of my head says I made the right choice! Oh, and you're welcome, by the way."

"For what?" Killjoy protests.

"If I hadn't shown up, you two would be toast."

Mad rolls her eyes. "My hero."

Suddenly, Killjoy raises her hand, signalling everyone to stop. "Mad, look."

Killjoy points at a large, open section of the factory where a commotion took place. Broken crates and fortune cookie packages litter the floor.

Mad takes her eyes off Calhoun and looks. The fake Swordsman takes advantage of the momentary distraction, grabs a nearby shelf, knocks it over on Mad, and runs for it.

Killjoy quickly pulls the shelf off Mad, but when her young companion is free, the fake Swordsman is gone.

Mad is unscathed but frustrated by Calhoun's escape.

"Son of a—! How does he keep getting away?"

"Not important right now," Killjoy reassures. "Mad, something important went down here." She picks up some dust from the area where the commotion took place. "Just over two days ago."

"Around the time my dad hired you," Mad chimes in, enthusiastically.

"Exactly. Look at the footprints. There were five… no, six people here. There was some kind of ruckus. One of them was ambushed and set upon by the others. He made his escape through that door."

Killjoy points to the back exit. Our heroes exit through the back and into the street, but it is just as empty as the rest of the block.

Killjoy takes out her magnifying glass and examines the ground. "The fleeing man was wounded, and he went that way." Killjoy points in a westward direction.

"How do you know he was wounded?" Mad asks, hesitantly

"Cause there's a trail of blood heading that way."

"Oh my God! Is it my dad? Was my dad hurt?"

"I can't tell if it was your dad by a bloodstain. I don't have the ingredients for an identification spell, nor do I have a forensics lab in my pocket. The best we can do is follow the blood trail."

"How are we going to do that? It's barely visible."

"Yeah, that's why I have to make a booty call."

Mad raises her eyebrows in confusion as Killjoy presses a button on her cell phone and holds the receiver to her ear. "Hey, Gar… Yeah, it's me… Um, an overcoat and a wide-brimmed hat. Why do you need to know that?" Mad shakes her head in disapproval. "Anyhoo, remember when you said to call if I needed anything? Yeah, I'm going to need Toby."

———

Moments later, The Witch, The Human, and The Cat race down the streets of Obscure. Killjoy runs ahead, being led by a big, dumb-looking vampire at the end of a leash.

"You use a vampire as a bloodhound?" Mad exclaims.

"No creature is better at following a blood trail," the Witch reassures her.

Within minutes, Toby leads our heroes to a familiar location. A sickening feeling begins to settle in the pit of Mad's stomach. "Oh no, this is my building. Our building. Something bad has happened to my dad."

"Don't lose hope, Mad. We're not done following Toby," Killjoy assures her.

They follow the dumb vamp to a service entrance on the side of the building. The door has a combination lock on it. Killjoy just points her broom at the lock and blows the door open.

The service entrance takes them down a flight of steps, and soon they find themselves in a sub-basement. It is immediately apparent that The Swordsman used this room as his base of operations. Many paintings and relics depicting his adventures adorn the walls. Equipment and other monster-fighting accoutrements are displayed on nearly every surface, and of course, the Heavenly Blade is in the middle of the room, jabbed into a big square block, like Excalibur.

Seeing the sword in person leaves Mad breathless. She momentarily forgets about all the anguish and worry she has felt for the past few days as she slowly approaches the Heavenly Blade. She raises her hand to touch its hilt as if some unknown force was drawing her to it.

Then, suddenly, she stops: something in her peripheral vision gets her attention. She turns to look. It's her dad!

Charles Chan stands on the other side of the room with his hand over his stomach, where he is wounded. His face curls into a smile the moment his daughter notices him.

"Baba!" She screams with unbridled joy.

Mad forgets about the sword and runs straight for her father.

"Mad — no!" Killjoy cries, but it is too late.

Mad runs right at Charles, expecting a warm embrace but instead feels the cold, chilling mist of walking right through a Ghost.

Mad freezes in place as the harsh realisation of what she just experienced fully sinks in. She drops to her knees and sobs in agony.

"Sorry, Mad." Killjoy's eyes glisten as she sheds light on this tragic moment. "It's the Ghost Vision. It hasn't worn off yet. I was afraid something like this would happen."

"Did you know?"

"That your father had passed? I had a theory, but I didn't want to say anything until I was sure."

"I'm sorry, my little lotus," Charles interrupts. "I didn't want you to find out this way. I never wanted you to feel this pain."

"The Rewinder!" Mad shouts in desperation.

Killjoy's eyes narrow in confusion. "What?"

"The thing you used to reverse time in my dad's office. Use it now to go back to before my dad was killed."

"Sorry, Mad." She takes out the Rewinder and puts it in Mad's hands. "It won't work. The Rewinder only affects inorganic matter. Witches are forbidden from bringing back the dead. You can try it if you like, but it would only affect the inanimate objects around you and nothing more."

Mad's expression changes from deep sadness to intense rage. "Who did this?"

"Pardon me?" Charles responds.

"Who killed you, Baba?" she demands.

"It was Loopin Shadows. He figured out who I was."

"The Squire?"

"No, child. That was merely misdirection. Loopin Shadows discovered that I am The Swordsman."

Killjoy's eyes widen with absolute shock. "Holy Hecate!"

Killjoy and Mad look around the room, and it is very apparent that the man in all the portraits is a younger and thinner Charles.

Mad focuses on an old photograph from the 1890s in which a young Charles is seen wearing The Swordsman's signature bowler hat while working on the railroads with other Chinese immigrants. "I… I don't understand how you could have existed for so long? Are you a Night Dweller?"

"No. I was as human as you, my love. I was going to live a short, uneventful life building the railroads of the American West, until one day, when something caught my eye out in the desert. It glistened in the sunlight with the brightest light I had ever seen. It was calling to me like a siren out at sea. There it was, the Heavenly Blade.

"I abandoned my post and gave in to its call, drawing closer and closer, knowing that it belonged to me even though I had never laid eyes on its intoxicating beauty before that moment. Soon the blade stood before me, embedded in the ground like the sword from the Arthurian Legend. I reached out, wrapped my fingers around its handle, and pulled it out of the ground with little to no effort. The moment would have been more glorious if I hadn't been interrupted by my rail masters. Those stupid, violent men threatened me with guns and knives. They told me to hand over the blade and get back to work, or they would cut off all my limbs and leave me to die out in the desert heat.

"Then suddenly, with the same ease as a child taking his first steps, I dispatched my former masters. Not a shot was fired; not a single knife contacted my skin. The blade gave me the knowledge and skill to subdue my attackers, and it was at that very moment that my fate was clear. I was The Swordsman, charged to walk the Earth and vanquish the monsters that plague humanity.

"Years and decades went by, and it was apparent that the blade had expanded my life span. As my loved ones would age and die, I didn't. I continued travelling the Earth and fighting evil until I came to Obscure, where I met your mother. She was my first Squire. She fought at my side for many years until the day God gave us you, my little lotus, and that was the day my first love was taken from me."

Mad picks up a picture of her mother, Gabriel Chan, a gorgeous Chinese woman with a strong resemblance to her.

"After that, my life of adventure didn't seem as important," Charles continues. "I lived to protect you and give you the happy, normal life I never had. I took on a new squire." Charles motions towards Hime.

Hime bows to his master. "You are my Person. You belong to me."

"Hime, you can see him?" Mad enquires.

"He's an animal. He could always see him," Killjoy reminds.

"Along with my new squire," Charles went on, "I also employed a decoy to appear in my stead when my presence was needed, but my skills were not. After all, the legend of The Swordsman was far more powerful than any ability bestowed upon me by The Heavenly Blade. And thus, I discovered the greatest secret identity; a guaranteed way to never be suspected as The Swordsman. I would simply pretend to be The Squire."

Realisation takes over Killjoy's face. "Brilliant. No one would ever suspect Robin of being Batman."

"Exactly," Charles agrees. "No one ever seeks to challenge the faithful assistant when there is more prestige to be had from defeating a legend."

"That still doesn't explain why you started aging."

"I found that the less I used the blade, the more I aged, and after fifteen years of choosing parenthood over the paranormal, I looked in the mirror and saw the pudgy old man who stands before you."

Mad is in deep thought for a moment until the words escape her throat.

"Shadows. He ambushed you and killed you, but how did he discover you were The Swordsman?'

"My decoy betrayed me."

Mad's brow furrows. "Calhoun."

As Charles explains the circumstances behind his demise, Killjoy reconstructs the murder scene in her mind. She sees the interior of the abandoned fortune cookie factory, but without the debris and disarray in which she saw it earlier. Instead, she sees Charles and Calhoun having what appears to be a friendly meeting.

Suddenly, one of the shutter gates for the loading dock rolls open. Loopin Shadows enters the abandoned edifice accompanied by Mason, Rip, and Torn. Charles quickly dives for his sword, which he left on a nearby table while speaking to Calhoun, but Shadows fires one of his finger darts at him, hitting the legendary hero right in the stomach. Charles grips himself around the middle and crashes through the table.

Killjoy sees Shadows thanking Calhoun for leading them there and hands him a fat envelope that the shady cop quickly pockets. Shadows smiles brightly, with his shark teeth on full display, as he points at Charles and gets ready to fire another finger dart.

Charles is ready this time. He swings the heavenly blade and cuts the dart in half in mid-flight. The volatile substance within the dart causes it to explode. The villains are knocked back, and debris flies everywhere. Pieces of wood and old fortune cookie packages slide across the floor and land in the exact configuration that Killjoy and Mad found earlier.

When the smoke clears, Charles is gone, and a trail of blood leading out through the back door is all that remains of him.

The villains follow.

Killjoy pauses the scene before her. All the players involved freeze in midmotion. She makes everything fade to black, leaving herself alone in an endless dark void. She then fades into another scene.

She is back in The Swordsman's lair, but she is alone. Right on cue, Charles stumbles in, dragging his sword behind him with one hand and gripping his middle with the other.

Hime enters and sees the condition of his master. The faithful Squire tries to approach him with concern, but Charles stops him.

"No!" Charles orders. "You know what to do. Only Kassandra Killjoy can help Madeline now. So if you truly wish to honour me, do as you were instructed."

Hime bows in respect. He slides his tiny head into a collar with the USB drive he would eventually deliver to Killjoy, and gets ready to leave.

"Squire!" Charles calls. Hime turns to face his master. "It was an honour to have served at your side."

Hime lovingly rubs his tiny body against his master's leg before vanishing into mid-air.

Now that Charles is alone, he clumsily walks to the big square stone in the middle of the room; the same chunk of rock where he found the sword embedded, out in the desert.

Charles takes his trusty weapon and reinserts it into the old piece of rock. He holds onto the sword's handle very tightly as he takes a moment to look at a photograph of him and Mad together.

"May destiny be kind to you, my little lotus. I love you."

He lets go of the sword's handle, and as soon as the protective effects of the blade are no longer affecting him, he is instantly enveloped in white and black flame.

Charles cries out for a brief moment as the bright white flames light the entire room, revealing his legacy's remnants around him. And just like that, the flames die down, and humanity's greatest champion is gone.

As Charles's ashes float before her, Killjoy pauses her vision. She wipes a tear off her face as her surroundings cross-dissolve into the present, and she's back in the room with Hime, Toby, Mad, and Charles' ghost.

Mad continues to question her father. "I still don't understand why you hid all of this from me."

"I fought for years under the misguided conclusion that I was going to just settle down with your mother and have a normal life one day," Charles explained. "And then she was gone, and I suddenly realised that I had wasted our time together seeking meaningless thrills. I was simply trying to give you the life I should have given her."

"But Baba, I—"

Suddenly, Toby the vampire starts growling like a dog sensing an intruder.

Killjoy turns to the dumb vampire. "What's wrong, Toby? What's wrong, boy?"

A chill runs down Mad's spine as she looks. "Killjoy, don't ask me how, but I feel like something terrible is about to—"

Toby the vampire sparks into black and white flames at that exact moment. Their faithful bloodhound is gone before Killjoy has a chance to put him out.

"Ah, damn! Garrett's going to be pissed off!" Killjoy protests.

"Sorry about that." A familiar, sinister voice comes from the doorway. "The little tyke was being too noisy for my taste."

They all turn toward the entryway to see Loopin Shadows enter the room.

The King of the Slashers is accompanied by his bodyguards, Mason and Torn, as well as Sergeant Calhoun and The Grand Witch herself, Minerva Madrigal.

"You son of a bitch, I will kill you!" Mad threatens.

Killjoy holds Mad back before she can take any further action.

"Stand down, ladies," Minerva commands. "You are outnumbered and outmatched."

Killjoy is exceptionally displeased to see the grand witch. "Minerva, I should have known you'd fall in with a scumbag like him."

"I do what is best for our kind, Kassandra. Mr Shadows makes a persuasive argument about the state of our world, and he is willing to provide a solution to change it for the better."

"And what would this solution be?" Mad questions.

"Yes, that is why I came down to this disgusting, dusty basement," Shadows responds sarcastically. "To reveal my evil plan to my nemesis and her trusty sidekick."

Mad is taken aback by his retort. "Sidekick?"

"You sanctimonious simpletons couldn't even begin to understand the intricate machinations of my—"

"You're going use The Nail of Nefario to make more Slashers," Killjoy concludes.

Shadows just stares at her, completely stunned. "But how did you. . ?"

"Oh, come on," Killjoy continues. "You're always pissing and moaning and whining and bitching about how Slashers are a minority and how unfair it is that you're ostracised in the monster world, blah, blah, blah, cry, cry, cry—"

"Enough!" he demands.

"I told you she'd eventually get under your skin," Minerva reminds him.

"Now, you can just create an army with a snap of your fingers and overtake the human world and eventually all the other Night Dweller clans," Killjoy further exposits.

Minerva realises Killjoy is correct, as the witch detective continues her deduction.

"After all, why just punish the lowly humans if you can finally get sweet revenge on the Night Dwellers who shunned you? How's that? Am I in the ballpark?"

"Yup, that's pretty much the guy's entire plan, Killjoy," Calhoun confirms.

Shadows eerily turns his attention towards the false swordsman. "Which reminds me. I am yet to compensate you for leading us here, Sergeant Calhoun."

Shadows shoots Calhoun with a gauntlet dart in a swift motion, and the dirty cop burns to death, enveloped in magical flames.

Satisfied with his work, Shadows begins to give Killjoy a slow sarcastic clap. "Congratulations, Ms Killjoy. You are as extraordinary a detective as they say you are. Anything else you'd like to add?"

"Yeah, you forgot one major detail to make your oh-so-brilliant plan work."

"And what is that?"

"The Nail of Nefario. You don't have it."

"Ah yes, which brings me to the real reason I came down to this shit hole. Ms, Madrigal, if you please?"

Minerva raises her hand at his command, and Hime flies through the air and into her hands.

"Hey lady, you're not my person. I don't like it when you touch my hairs."

She holds up the small feline by his neck and points a long dagger directly at his left eye. "Give us the Nail of Nefario or I will gouge his eyes out and eat them."

Killjoy is appalled by the threat. "Ew, graphic much."

"Put him down, you old hag!" Mad demands. "You're wasting your time. We don't have the stupid Nail of Nefario."

Shadows rolls his eyes at the young woman's claim.

"Come on, Ms Killjoy. Everyone in this room knows you already figured this out, except for your human pet. So stop playing dumb. It doesn't suit you."

Killjoy lets out an exasperated breath as Mad realises.

"Wait, you know where it is?"

"Yeah, I've known since yesterday," Killjoy confesses. "Your dad put it where you'd keep it safe, and no one would look."

Killjoy pulls Mad's skateboard from the straps of her backpack. She tears off the wheel that broke off the last two times Mad had an accident. She pulls the screw that is supposed to be holding the wheel in place, revealing it to be The Nail of Nefario.

She holds it out to Shadows.

He takes it from her with uncontainable delight. "And my horoscope said today was going to be a bad day. All right, kill them!"

His minions get ready to execute his orders when Minerva suddenly stops them.

"Don't be hasty, Mr Shadows. Kassandra might be lying."

Shadows signals his minions to stop. Both Mason and Torn freeze in their tracks.

"Let's wait until after you perform the ritual," Minerva advises. "Once we are successful and we know for sure that this is the real Nail of Nefario, we will no longer have any need for them, and then we can all take turns killing them in unique and amusing ways."

"Well, when you're right, you're right," Shadows relented. "Bring them along."

Mason and Torn grab Killjoy and Mad.

"And the Blade," Minerva suggests. "Perhaps we should bring it along. We wouldn't want the next chosen one to stumble by, get chosen, and ruin our plans."

Shadows considers her suggestion with faint concern on his face, but he shakes it off as he issues his response.

"You're right. The Blade should be within sight to ensure the success of the expansion."

Minerva enchants the sword, stone and all, and levitates it, making the evil-fighting relic follow her out of the room.

Killjoy and Mad are dragged along by Shadow's minions.

Mad struggles with every step. "Where are you taking us, you disgusting freaks?"

"If Shadows is going to make more Slashers, he will need lots of evil douche bags," Killjoy reminds Mad.

"So?"

"So, where do we keep all the evil douchebags in this town?"

Chapter 8

Peril at Preston Penitentiary

In a town filled with ghouls and monsters, there is no more terrifying a location than Preston Penitentiary; a Supermax facility meant to contain the most depraved and unforgivable members of human society. Ironically, its owner, the beloved billionaire Light Preston, is the most deserving of being housed in such a facility; he is better known in the underworld as Loopin Shadows.

The King of the Slashers leads Killjoy, Mad, and the others into the main detention centre of the facility. "Ladies and gentlemen. Welcome to Preston Penitentiary. Purchased fifty years ago by Yours Truly for just this occasion. You will all be a part of history tonight, as we witness a new beginning for Night Dwellers and the Slasher Clan." He turns to his minions. "Mason, if you would be so kind as to show our guests to their room, so we can begin the expansion of our race."

Mason picks up Killjoy and Mad like ragdolls, carries them down a long hallway and forces them into a small room.

Minerva follows them in. "Ladies, I hope you find your current accommodation to your liking."

"What?" Killjoy barks. "I specifically asked for two twin beds and a beach-side view. I'm going to give you such a bad Yelp review!"

"Oh child, you're always so amusing."

Torn puts a pair of iron manacles around Killjoy's wrists. The manacles appear to be enchanted as they snap open, and iron tendrils hold Killjoy's arms against her body and then close an iron ring around her neck, leaving her unable to move her arms or turn her head."

"You're not going to get out of this one, you half-breed witch," Torn informs her.

"You cost me, my sister. So when this is over, I will cut you to pieces, personally."

"Okay, the turn-down service sucks. I'm seriously considering spending the night at a motel."

"Joke all you want," Minerva interjects. "In eleven minutes, this will all be over."

Torn throws Hime into the cell, bound and gagged. The little creature struggles to get free but can't. Mad comforts him to the best of her abilities.

Satisfied with the state of their captives, Minerva and Torn take their leave, slamming the cell door behind them.

"Huh, she told us exactly how much time before the ritual begins. Interesting," Killjoy muses. "Mad — you okay over there?"

"Yeah, I'm great. My dad was killed by a psychotic Freddy Kruger wannabe, the world's about to end, and I'm in jail."

"It could be worse."

"How? How could it possibly be worse?"

"They could be releasing another Fast and Furious movie."

Mad smiles. "Don't make me laugh, Killjoy. I don't want to laugh right now."

"Mad, that's what we do. We laugh in the face of danger."

"No, you laugh in the face of danger. You're the monster-fighting detective witch; I'm just the dumb ass in distress."

"Is that what you think? Mad, this is not my hero's journey. It's yours."

"What are you talking about?"

Killjoy is legitimately surprised at her lack of awareness. "I can't believe you haven't figured this out! Remember when we were spying on Shadows at the Court of Darkness, and he said that he would get rid of The Swordsman for them?"

"Yeah, and he did. He killed my dad."

"Yeah, he killed your dad before he made that claim." Mad realises there's logic in Killjoy's words. "Now, do you remember what Minerva said when she talked Shadows into bringing the sword along?" Killjoy asks.

"They shouldn't leave it lying around for someone else to come by and get chosen."

"Exactly, The Swordsman doesn't die with your father. Someone else picks up the sword and continues the legacy."

A sense of clarity takes over Mad's face. "Oh my God! That's why he wanted to keep me away from this world. He knew!"

"And the moment you walked into that room and laid eyes on The Heavenly Blade, you knew it, too. Now say it."

"I'm The Swordsman!" Mad looks through the bars of her cell and sees Mason guarding the sword just a few feet away.

"Well, Swordswoman — but you call yourself whatever you want."

"This has to be some kind of mistake. I'm tiny and weak and—"

"The daughter of two of the greatest warriors of our time: The Swordsman and his Squire. It's in your blood."

"But the sword is still way over there, out of my reach. We're locked in here, you're without your powers, and we have no way of getting out. So even if I 'accepted my sacred duty,' there's no way I could—"

"Mad, check your pocket."

"What are you—?"

"Shut up and check your pocket."

Mad reaches into her jeans pockets and finds Killjoy's Rewinder.

Killjoy looks at her with a confident smirk. "You're fresh out of excuses, Mad. Will you accept the calling, cross the threshold, and conclude your Hero's Journey? Or stay in this cell and continue to be a so-called dumb ass in distress?"

"Ah, what the hell. I did promise Shadows I'd kill him."

"That's the spirit!"

Mad holds the Rewinder over Killjoy's manacles, presses the button. "Tempo Reversa."

The display on the Rewinder starts to count down to zero, and the manacles reverse themselves to the moment before they were locked around Killjoy's wrists. The heavy bonds fall off her arms and hit the ground.

Magical energy surges all over Killjoy's hands. "That's much better. Okay, before you cross that threshold, you'll need this." Killjoy pulls out The Swordsman's bowler hat from her coat.

"My Dad's stupid old hat?"

"Hey, that hat started as a sign of servitude, and your father turned it into a symbol that struck fear in the hearts of all Night Dwellers. The Heavenly Blade will give you power, but the legend of The Swordsman will make you invincible."

Mad smiles and accepts the hat from Killjoy. She puts it on and stands back. "How do I look?"

"Like a big damn Hero. Now let's get to work." Killjoy holds her hand out, and her broom magically appears.

The cell door gets blown open with a green plasma bolt. Killjoy and Mad heroically emerge from the smoke.

They see Mason at the end of the hallway, guarding the sword.

"You got this?" Killjoy asks.

"Maybe."

"Not as reassuring as a 'yes', but not as bad as a 'no'. Good luck. Come on, Hime." She snaps her fingers, and Hime's bonds fall off.

"I follows you, lady," the talking cat responds as he takes off after Killjoy down a second hallway, leaving Mad on her own.

The new Swordsman starts walking towards Mason, alone. *Oh God, Oh God! What am I doing? What am I doing?*

You're accepting your destiny, little lotus. The voice of her father responded within her mind.

"Dad? Is that you?"

"Of course."

"The child tears must still be working."

"I'm always with you, dear. Now focus."

"Dad, that seven-foot behemoth is going to kill me."

"That's what they want you to think," Charles reassures. "Night Dwellers always want to fool you into thinking they're bigger, stronger, and more powerful."

"They are."

"They're not! You're The Swordsman; you're not afraid of monsters. Monsters are afraid of you."

Mad is overtaken by confidence and addresses Mason directly.

"Hey ugly!"

Mason notices her, and he is not pleased. "Hey! How you get out of your cell?"

"I'm going to need that." Mad points at the sword perched on its rock right behind him. "So move or be moved."

"Stupid hat, Girl." Mason goes to crush her with both of his fists.

Mad quickly dodges his attack with a shoulder roll between the giant monster's legs and ends up right in front of the sword.

Before Mason can figure out where she went, Mad grabs the sword. The moment her fingers wrap around the handle, cold air rushes through her lungs, and the world around her decelerates to super-slow motion.

She can see Merlin and the seven Sorcerers crafting the Heavenly Blade. She can see all the Swordsmen that came before her, but more importantly, she can see, beyond a shadow of a doubt, that she is The Swordsman now.

She pulls the sword out of the rock, and a blinding light shoots in every direction. Mason shields his eyes. When the light subsides, Mad stands before Mason holding the sword and ready for battle.

"Any advice, Baba?"

"Kick his ass."

The big, dumb monster roars and charges at her like a rhino. Mad stands her ground. Mason gets closer and closer.

Suddenly, Mad throws the Blade straight up into the air and takes one step back.

Mason is confused by her unorthodox move and comes to a screeching halt right in front of her. Before he can question why she threw away her weapon, the sword comes back down on top of his head, impaling itself through the top of his skull.

The Slasher drops to his knees. Mad pulls the sword from his head as he falls dead on his face.

"Consider yourself moved," Mad quips.

"Very clever, little lotus," Charles compliments.

"*Xie xie*, Baba."

Torn rounds the corner and sees Mason's corpse at Mad's feet at that exact moment.

Without hesitation, she draws her sickle blades and runs right at Mad.

"Need help, little lotus?" Charles offers.

"Nah, I got this."

Mad gets to work. She quickly dodges Torn's attacks and blocks all of her offence. Torn gets more frustrated with every repetition.

"Who do you think you are to challenge me like this? You are nobody, you are—"

Then, in the blink of an eye, Mad shatters both of Torn's sickle blades and runs her through with her sword. Torn is shocked by the sight of her death wound.

"I am Mad Chan, The Swordsman."

Mad pulls the sword out of Torn and watches her crumple to the ground. "Baba, if this is the last time I talk to you, I promise to honour your legacy and make you proud."

"You already have."

Mad holds back the tears, puts her game face back on, and takes off at full speed down the hallway.

Killjoy and Hime arrive at Preston Penitentiary's security room at that very moment.

"Watch the door, Hime," the Witch instructs. "If anyone who's not one of your persons comes along, teleport them to the boiler room."

"Okay, lady." The feline responds as he takes a defensive stance in the doorway.

Killjoy walks over to the three dozen security monitors mounted along the entire left side of the room. She can see Mad walking away after defeating Mason and Torn, and Shadows making a speech in the main detention centre.

The Witch smiles as she begins casting a spell on the monitor with Shadows on it. When her work is done, Shadows appears to be in his human form from the monitor's point of view.

Oh, this is going to be so much fun later.

With her first task completed, Killjoy now moves over to the window, which is secured with metal bars. Killjoy knocks the bars out of her way with a quick plasma bolt and jumps out of the smoking hole she leaves behind.

Outside the building, Killjoy's broom carries her to the rooftop, where she lands swiftly and approaches a stone gargoyle perched on a corner. "Stand to attention, soldier; I have an errand for thee."

The gargoyle responds aggressively. "Know thy place, witch. I shall not take orders from a Night Dweller, nor will I interfere in thy matters unless humans are at risk."

"Hold thy tongue, knave! I am only half a Night Dweller, and it is my human half that requires your aid."

"Very well, then. What is thy command?" he says, begrudgingly.

"First of all, what's with the old English? It's the twenty-first century. Get with the times. And secondly, I need you to deliver a message to Detective Lancaster of the ninety-ninth precinct."

———

Back inside, Shadows stands in the middle of the detention centre, delivering a seemingly endless speech surrounded by cells containing the worst criminals in the country.

"Glorious day, my soon-to-be kin. You can't have a revolution without evolution, and today is the day you evolve into so much more than mere men. Today is the day you join a superior race and you will stand tall above all others…"

His speech goes on and on as Mad watches from a catwalk above. Killjoy joins her soon after that.

"Did you get it done?" Mad asks.

"Yup. If we fail, we'll at least have a plan B."

"Suggestion: let's not fail."

"Good suggestion. I'll take it into serious consideration. Ah balls, Mr. Chatty-Pants is about done with his epic speech."

"...So say goodbye to your lives of mediocrity," Shadows continues, "and say hello to an eternity in the glory of the Slasher Clan!" The Slasher lifts the Nail of Nefario high above his head and plunges it into his chest.

Purple energy begins bursting out in every direction. The inmates within the cells get hit with purple light beams and transform into ghastly and disturbing Slashers. Shadows laugh maniacally in his triumph.

He laughs so hard that he fails to notice Mad drop down into a kneeling position on the other side of the room.

Minerva, however, notices her immediately. The Grand Witch confronts the new Swordsman. She draws her broom and fires a plasma bolt right at Mad.

Mad reveals the Heavenly Blade she has been holding behind her. Minerva's eyes widen as she watches Mad take the sword like a baseball bat and swat at the plasma bolt. Mad knocks the bolt in the opposite direction.

Minerva watches in horror as the bolt flies past her and towards Shadows.

"Loopin!" the Witch shouts in vain.

Shadows looks down just in time to see the plasma bolt make contact his explosive gauntlet. His smile fades.

Boom!

A black and white fireball fills the room.

The effects of the Nail of Nefario cease as everyone gets knocked away in different directions.

Minerva is the first to rise from under some collapsed concrete. "Bloody amateurs! That's the last time I work with a bunch of filthy—"

Before she can finish that thought, she gets hit by a green plasma bolt that knocks her right into the wall.

Killjoy stands on the opposite side of the room, holding her broom like a shotgun.

"Hey, Minerva! It's been a minute, hasn't it? You want to catch up over a cup of coffee?"

Minerva gets up and does her best to collect herself. "You meddlesome brat!"

"I learned from the best."

Minerva draws her broom and the two clash using their brooms as quarterstaffs.

At this time, Shadows rises from the wreckage, missing an arm, but within seconds a new one grows in its place. "Ah, that's much better."

A white plasma bolt hits the wall behind him, completely missing him.

He turns to see Mad holding the Heavenly Blade like a rifle.

"Wow!" she says. "I didn't know the sword could do that! Anyway, consider that a warning shot, Shadows. Now stand down."

"A warning shot?" he laughed. "You stupid child!"

But before he can take action against his new enemy, Hime appears before him in a defensive stance. "Hey, deh stinky feets. That's my person; she belongs to me."

"First, I will kill your pet, and then—" Hime vanishes before Shadows can get a hold of him. "What the—?"

The teleporting feline reappears on his shoulder. He again tries to grab the cat but catches nothing but air.

Mad watches, completely delighted by Shadow's continuous failure. Finally, Hime appears on a control panel behind him. He once again lunges at the little creature, but it teleports away. Shadows crashes into the wall, accidentally hitting the release button for all the cells.

All the metal doors swing open, and his newly created army begins to emerge.

Hime reappears, hiding behind Mad's legs.

Shadows laughs wickedly. "How delightfully appropriate that the first victim in our war against humanity will be The Swordsman."

"Hey, dumbass — how are you going to control your army without this?" Mad holds up the Nail of Nefario.

Shadows quickly checks his chest and discovers that it is not there. Worry takes over his face.

Mad's body relaxes into a very cocky stance. "You just turned two dozen of the evilest bastards on the planet into freaks, and I guarantee you that their first desire will not be to join The Slasher Clan."

Shadows addresses the inmates, "Brothers, don't be hasty, I—"

The newly created slashers quickly jump on Shadows and begin to attack him, brutally.

Mad slips the Nail of Nefario into her pocket and turns to check on Killjoy. She sees the witch detective fighting her arch-nemesis and quickly gaining the upper hand.

"Yo! Killjoy, wrap it up!" Mad instructs.

Killjoy nods and throws her enchanted pocket watch at Minerva. The chain wraps itself around the grand witch, and soon she is pulled across the room and crash-lands right in front of Mad. The new Swordsman takes out the iron cuffs used on Killjoy earlier and puts them on Minerva.

"No!" the grand witch exclaims.

"Turnabout is fair play, Biotch!" Mad replies.

Killjoy walks up and pats her on the shoulder. "Good job, Swordsman."

"Not so bad yourself, paranormal private-eye."

But their praise is cut short by Minerva. "How dare you gloat, you prattling harpies!"

Killjoy and Mad turn to see Shadows covered in blood and standing over the bodies of all the new slashers. "Today was supposed to be a beautiful day. And look at what you meddlesome shrews made me do! I am wearing the blood of my brothers when I should be wearing yours."

"You want our blood? Then come and get it, douche bag!" Mad invites.

Killjoy is impressed by her bravado. "Damn, Mad — badass!"

"Thank you."

Shadows draws a collapsible axe from the remains of his coat, and without any further warning, attacks them. Killjoy and Mad fight in beautiful tandem, keeping the vile Slasher at bay.

A stray plasma bolt knocks Shadow's silver mask away, revealing that he isn't hiding scars, but half of his face is permanently stuck in human form.

Mad's jaw drops at the horrific sight. "So the part of your face you keep hidden is the part that looks like Jon Hamm?"

"Now that's a twist M. Night Shyamalan wouldn't see coming!" Killjoy quips.

Enraged by their disrespect, Shadows becomes more savage with his attacks and eventually kicks Killjoy right through a stone column, knocking her out.

Mad lunges forward with her sword, but Shadows evades the attack, causing the Swordsman to stab the wall. Shadows drives her to the ground with a chokeslam, leaving the sword in the wall.

Mad has the wind knocked out of her, and she is too busy gasping for air to evade Shadows' next attack. The Slasher picks her up by the front of her shirt and brings her very close to his face.

"What are you without your witch and your sword? You are nothing! You have nothing!"

"I still have this."

Mad holds up the Nail of Nefario, and before Shadows has a chance to react, she plunges the magical spike into her chest, and immediately purple energy bolts begin to shoot out.

Shadows tries to run, but he is just too close, and a stray bolt catches him in the back.

Killjoy wakes up just in time to see this. She quickly grabs Minerva and tries to drag her away from the purple bolts, but with Minerva's dead weight, they are moving too slowly, and The Nail's effects are getting closer and closer.

Killjoy trips and Minerva's body falls right over her legs, pinning her down. She reaches for her broom, but it doesn't answer her call. She is confused by the malfunction for just a moment, but then remembers that Minerva is wearing iron shackles.

"The Iron! Oh no, I'm too close!"

Horrified, the witch detective accepts her fate and shields her face from the transformative energy bolts heading her way. Suddenly, Hime lands on top of her and Minerva and teleports them away just in time. The energy fully envelops the room.

Killjoy opens her eyes to find that she, Minerva, and Hime are now back on the prison's roof.

"Oy!" the stone gargoyle calls out. "You ain't back for another favour, are you?"

Killjoy ignores the rude sentry and turns to face her teleporting cat. "Oh, you are going to get so many tunas."

"In my mouff."

Meanwhile, back in the main detention centre, all the dead slashers revert to their human form under the effects of the Nail. And then, just as quickly as the energy storm began, it ends with Mad pulling the nail from her chest, leaving a terrible wound.

She drops the Nail of Nefario to the ground, holds the wound with one hand, and reaches for her sword with the other. The moment her fingers wrap around the Heavenly Blade, white light engulfs her entire body, and her wounds are healed.

"Thank God that worked."

Shadows wakes up and sees his reflection in a broken piece of glass on the ground. He's human. "No. No!"

Mad stands by, satisfied with her work. "Try hiding your human side now, Ahole!"

To her surprise, the villain bows before her. "Benevolent Swordsman tried and true, grant this villain a swift death."

"I have to respectfully decline," Mad answers.

"But you said you'd kill me!"

"No, I said I would kill Loopin Shadows, and I did. He's gone. I have no beef with Light Preston. He's just a rich douche bag that now has to live with the indignity of being human. Not to mention the humiliation of getting knocked out by a ninety-pound girl."

"What?"

Mad punches him right across the face. Preston hits the ground pathetically.

Mad shakes her hand, feeling the consequences. "Ouch! Punching hurts!"

"Yeah, sorry about that," Killjoy says as she walks up, handing her an ice pack from her coat.

Mad puts the pack on her hand.

"If it's any consolation, it looked cool," Killjoy assures.

They walk over to Minerva, and Mad removes the manacles.

"You're letting me go?" the Grand Witch questions.

"We promise not to breathe a word of your involvement to the Holy Alliance," Killjoy negotiates, "as long as you swear not to align yourself with more extremists."

"We already lost one member of The Court of Darkness to that jerk wad," Mad adds. "There's no sense in losing two."

"Deal?" Killjoy holds out her hand

Minerva takes an exasperated breath. "Deal."

Minerva and Killjoy shake hands. With this, the Grand Witch goes to leave.

"Oh, and Minerva…" Mad detains her. The Witch turns to face The Swordsman. "If you step out of line one more time, I'm going to put this sword through your face."

Minerva nods and takes her leave.

"You dumb harpies!" Light Preston shouts.

"Damn, I thought I knocked him out," Mad says, disappointed.

"You think you've won…"

"Yeah, pretty much," Killjoy proclaims.

"I'm rich, you ignorant floosies! You think I'm bad? Wait until you meet my lawyers!"

Suddenly the doors burst open, and dozens of police officers flood the room. Preston's confidence lessens. The officers surround Preston and instruct him not to move.

Soon Detective Lankaster enters, followed by a short, bald, pudgy man.

The detective addresses the businessman formally. "Good morning, Mr. Preston. We received a rather disturbing anonymous tip claiming that you broke into this prison in the middle of the night and started slaughtering the inmates with an axe."

Preston is outraged. "That's preposterous. What proof do you—"

Lankaster looks down at the corpses at his feet and the bloody axe next to him.

Officers immediately move in and handcuff the former Slasher.

"Proof?" The pudgy man chimes in. "I have surveillance footage of you murdering these men, you sick—"

"It's okay, Warden," Lankaster interrupts. "We'll make sure justice is served."

"When you called me to tell me what I might find here today," the Warden begins, "I thought it was a demented prank, but thank God I listened; otherwise I would have shown up this morning and found this!" He gestures toward all the corpses, shocked.

"I was the one who called in the tip-off, Warden," Killjoy speaks up as she and Mad stepped forward, dressed in professional business suits.

"And who are you, young lady?"

"Ah, this is private investigator Kassandra Killjoy," Lankaster explains, "and her assistant Madeline Chan. They're friends of the department."

They shake hands with the warden.

"How'd you get mixed up in this, Killjoy?" Lankaster asks.

"I was helping Mad look into the disappearance of her father. When I found evidence that Mr Preston might be involved, I followed him here and stumbled onto this horror show."

Preston's rage builds. "Oh, you think you're so clever, you stupid little—"

"Get him out of here!" Lankaster demands.

Officers drag him away.

"All right, boys, let's lock the crime scene down and call the meat wagon. We have many bodies to move. Warden, please accompany Lieutenant Cline and give him your full statement."

Everyone jumps into action as Lankaster turns to Killjoy and Mad. "You will tell me what actually went down, later, over a cup of coffee, right?"

"You got it," Killjoy assures.

Lankaster turns to Mad. "See, kid, I told you we'd take care of you."

"Thanks."

They shake hands.

"And good luck with your new job."

Mad smiles as she, Killjoy, and Hime take their leave.

Chapter 9

Another End and New Beginnings

The sun shines over Obscure City, effectively hiding the city's sinister side. Even the cemetery seems inviting, as our heroes meet in the Mausoleum of Heroes to pay respects to the fallen Swordsman, Charles Chan. A new marble casket has been erected in his honour.

Mad lights some incense, and Killjoy and Hime offer a deep bow, out of respect.

"You know, I saw him in action once, a few decades ago," Killjoy breaks the silence. "Never thought I'd be a part of his legend."

"Still feels weird to be taking on such a dangerous role," Mad thinks aloud. "He was so overprotective; he would lose his mind any time he saw me riding my skateboard without a helmet."

"We are never who our parents expect us to be. My dad didn't want me to be a witch, and my mom didn't want me to be a detective, and somehow, I found a way to disappoint them both. Oh, and speaking of disappointments… Are you sure you're not interested in being my assistant? I could use the extra muscle."

"Nah, you were right. I was never meant to be a sidekick. I'm going to try the lone-hero thing for a bit, or at least until I find my own Squire. Thanks for hijacking my dad's, by the way." Mad gestures toward Hime.

"Hey, I was protecting Hime. Naming him my familiar was the best way to get the Lycan Clan to leave him alone."

"Fine, fine. Any word on Shadows — I mean, Preston?"

"Oh, he's going to be in jail for the rest of his natural life. I extended the glimmer cast over the city to the surveillance footage. So any human who looks at it only sees Light Preston killing inmates. No Loopin Shadows, no slashers, no witches…"

"… No Swordsman. Got it. Thank you for everything, Killjoy."

Mad offers her hand for a handshake.

"It was my pleasure, Mad."

The two shake hands and go their separate ways.

Hime jumps on Killjoy's shoulder, and they vanish into thin air.

Moments later, The Witch and her Familiar re-appear on the sidewalk adjacent to Killjoy Komics. The Paranormal Private Eye monologues to herself as they walk towards the building. *All's well that ends well. A mystery solved, a villain in jail, and Obscure City has a new Champion to protect it. Hopefully, I can take a little break from fighting monsters and…*

Killjoy notices that her front door has been forced open…. *no rest for weary, I guess.*

Killjoy draws her broom as Hime gets on guard. They enter the building slowly and cautiously. "Whoever you are, I'm impressed. Very few can override my protection spells."

She suddenly notices Dan The-Comic-Book-Man, frozen in place. She checks his pulse. She exhales with relief when she detects that he's alive. "Petrification spell — again, impressed. So how about you stop impressing me and start introducing yourself."

An elegant, statuesque woman in black shades steps out of the shadows.

Killjoy is very surprised by the identity of the intruder.

"Icarus Lawren! What is the leader of the Silent Knights doing in my store? Did you hear about our excellent selection of back issues?"

"My apologies for the theatrics, Ms Killjoy," Lawren begins, "but I wanted to make sure to get your attention."

"I'm listening." About a dozen angels with swords appear around Lawren. "I'm listening intently."

"The Holy Alliance would like to recruit you, officially," Lauren offers. "Our new Swordsman might need your assistance. "

"All Mad has to do is ask. So what's with the formal visit?"

"She might not understand the gravity of the upcoming threat."

"Upcoming threat?"

"We have reason to believe that we might see the return of The Original Seven."

Killjoy's eyes go wide, and her shoulders drop. Her broom slips out of her hand and hits the ground with a resounding thud.

"Merciful Malus!"

EPILOGUE

Night falls over Obscure, and the city reverts to its macabre state. More noticeably so at the Court of Darkness, where its six remaining members meet again.

Minerva Madrigal is escorted into the room by a couple of very large very intimidating guards. The rest of the court members sit around the table, looking rather displeased.

The vampire Callus begins the meeting. "I understand we will no longer need to worry about Mr. Shadows or any other Slashers making their way into our sacred circle."

"Yes, your majesty." Minerva answers. "Loopin Shadows is no longer a threat. I made sure to sabotage his plans at every turn."

"Oh, I love it when you're devious. Please tell us how did it?" Veil requests. "I'm dying to know how you fooled some disgusting Slasher."

The others nod in agreement.

"First, I tricked the fool into sparing Kassandra and Chan by making him believe they were somehow more valuable alive. I also talked him into bringing The Heavenly Blade to the penitentiary, where it would be well within Chan's reach. Then I provided Chan a means of escape by allowing her to keep the Rewinder device that was clearly in her pocket. Last but not least, my personal favourite, I redirected a plasma bolt that I fired at Chan to hit Shadow's unnecessarily dangerous gauntlet."

"And he still believed in your alliance?" Callus wonders.

"Never doubted it for a moment."

"Well then, take your seat, Grand Witch."

Minerva does as instructed.

Professor Pretorius, however, remains dissatisfied. "Pardon my belligerence, Minerva, but Killjoy is still a threat. Look at how easily she uncovered Shadows' scheme and positioned the Swordsman to eliminate him. If she ever were to turn her attention on us..."

"My dear Professor, you need not worry." Minerva reassured. "I can personally guarantee that Kassandra Killjoy will never challenge this court. After all, I think I've proven that I am very good at manipulating my daughter."

Kassandra Killjoy
will return in
The Caskets of Chaos